TANDEM

The Monster Men

Professor Maxon and von Horn were standing over one of the six vats that stood under their heavy glass covers in the laboratory.

"What of these who are so imperfect?" asked von Horn. "You cannot take them into civilisation, nor would it be right to leave them here upon this island. What will you do with them?"

"I have given the matter but little thought," the professor said. "They are but the accidents of my great work. When I am gone they must look to themselves. It is unfortunate that they are as they are, but without them I could never have reached the perfection that I am sure we are to find here. And this is but the beginning." He passed his hand caressingly over the coffin-like vat at the head of which was a placard bearing the words *Number Thirteen*.

"But the others, Professor," insisted von Horn. "They are things! They are not human ... they are not even beast. They are terrible, soulless creatures. They are a constant and growing menace to us all, but most of all to your daughter."

A cunning look came into the professor's eyes. "I understand," he said. "You would rid yourself of rival suitors. But no! I shall not be thwarted in my cherished plan. Be this one what he may he shall wed my daughter!"

Edgar Rice Burroughs has also written:

THE PELLUCIDAR SERIES
At the Earth's Core
Pellucidar
Tanar of Pellucidar
Back to the Stone Age
Land of Terror
Savage Pellucidar

THE MOON SERIES
The Moon Maid
The Moon Men

THE CAPRONA SERIES
The Land that Time Forgot
The People that Time Forgot
Out of Time's Abyss
AND
Beyond the Farthest Star

These books are available in Tandem editions

The Monster Men

Edgar Rice Burroughs

TANDEM

published by
WYNDHAM PUBLICATIONS

Published in the United States by
Ace Books Inc.

A Tandem Book published in Great Britain in 1976 by
Wyndham Publications Ltd.

This edition follows the text of the first hardcover
book edition, originally published in 1929

Tandem Books are published by Tandem Publishing Ltd,
123 King Street, London W6 9JG
A Howard & Wyndham Company

Made and printed in Great Britain by
Hazell Watson & Viney Ltd, Aylesbury, Bucks

I

THE RIFT

As he dropped the last grisly fragment of the dismembered and mutilated body into the small vat of nitric acid that was to devour every trace of the horrid evidence which might easily send him to the gallows, the man sank weakly into a chair and throwing his body forward upon his great, teak desk buried his face in his arms, breaking into dry, moaning sobs.

Beads of perspiration followed the seams of his high, wrinkled forehead, replacing the tears which might have lessened the pressure upon his overwrought nerves. His slender frame shook, as with ague, and at times was racked by a convulsive shudder. A sudden step upon the stairway leading to his workshop brought him trembling and wide eyed to his feet, staring fearfully at the locked and bolted door.

Although he knew perfectly well whose the advancing footsteps were, he was all but overcome by the madness of apprehension as they came softly nearer and nearer to the barred door. At last they halted before it, to be followed by a gentle knock.

'Daddy!' came the sweet tones of a girl's voice.

The man made an effort to take a firm grasp upon himself that no tell-tale evidence of his emotion might be betrayed in his speech.

'Daddy!' called the girl again, a trace of anxiety in her voice this time. 'What *is* the matter with you, and what *are* you doing? You've been shut up in that hateful old room for three days now without a morsel to eat, and in all likelihood without a wink of sleep. You'll kill yourself with your stuffy old experiments.'

The man's face softened.

'Don't worry about me, sweetheart,' he replied in a well controlled voice. 'I'll soon be through now – soon be through – and then we'll go away for a long vacation – for a long vacation.'

'I'll give you until noon, Daddy,' said the girl in a voice which carried a more strongly defined tone of authority than her father's soft drawl, 'and then I shall come into that room, if I have to use an axe, and bring you out – do you understand?'

Professor Maxon smiled wanly. He knew that his daughter was equal to her threat.

'All right, sweetheart, I'll be through by noon for sure – by noon for sure. Run along and play now, like a good little girl.'

Virginia Maxon shrugged her shapely shoulders and shook her head hopelessly at the forbidding panels of the door.

'My dolls are all dressed for the day,' she cried, 'and I'm tired of making mud pies – I want you to come out and play with me.' But Professor Maxon did not reply – he had returned to view his grim operations, and the hideousness of them had closed his ears to the sweet tones of the girl's voice.

As she turned to retrace her steps to the floor below Miss Maxon still shook her head.

'Poor old Daddy,' she mused, 'were I a thousand years old, wrinkled and toothless, he would still look upon me as his baby girl.'

If you chance to be an alumnus of Cornell you may recall Professor Arthur Maxon, a quiet, slender, white-haired gentleman, who for several years was an assistant professor in one of the departments of natural science. Wealthy by inheritance, he had chosen the field of education for his life work solely from a desire to be of some material benefit to mankind since the meager salary which accompanied his professorship was not of sufficient import to influence him in the slightest degree.

Always keenly interested in biology, his almost unlimited means had permitted him to undertake, in secret, a series of daring experiments which had carried him so far in advance of the biologists of his day that he had, while others were still groping blindly for the secret of life, actually reproduced by chemical means the great phenomenon.

Fully alive to the gravity and responsibilities of his marvellous discovery he had kept the results of his experimentation, and even the experiments themselves, a profound secret not only from his colleagues, but from his only daughter, who heretofore had shared his every hope and aspiration.

It was the very success of his last and most pretentious effort that had placed him in the horrifying predicament in which he

6

now found himself – with the corpse of what was apparently a human being in his workshop and no available explanation that could possibly be acceptable to a matter-of-fact and unscientific police.

Had he told them the truth they would have laughed at him. Had he said: 'This is not a human being that you see, but the remains of a chemically produced counterfeit created in my own laboratory,' they would have smiled, and either hanged him or put him away with the criminally insane.

This phase of the many possibilities which he had realized might be contingent upon even the partial success of his work alone had escaped his consideration, so that the first wave of triumphant exultation with which he had viewed the finished result of this last experiment had been succeeded by overwhelming consternation as he saw the thing which he had created gasp once or twice with the feeble spark of life with which he had endowed it, and expire – leaving upon his hands the corpse of what was, to all intent and purpose, a human being, albeit a most grotesque and mis-shapen thing.

Until nearly noon Professor Maxon was occupied in removing the remaining stains and evidences of his gruesome work, but when he at last turned the key in the door of his workshop it was to leave behind no single trace of the successful result of his years of labor.

The following afternoon found him and Virginia crossing the station platform to board the express for New York. So quietly had their plans been made that not a friend was at the train to bid them farewell – the scientist felt that he could not bear the strain of attempting explanations at this time.

But there were those there who recognized them, and one especially who noted the lithe, trim figure and beautiful face of Virginia Maxon, though he did not know even the name of the professor. It was a tall well built young man who nudged one of his younger companions as the girl crossed the platform to enter her Pullman.

'I say, Dexter,' he exclaimed, 'who is that beauty?'

The one addressed turned in the direction indicated by his friend.

'By jove!' he exclaimed. 'Why it's Virginia Maxon and the Professor, her father. Now where do you suppose they're going?'

'I don't know – now,' replied the first speaker, Townsend J. Harper, Jr., in a half whisper, 'but I'll bet you a new car that I find out.'

A week later, with failing health and shattered nerves, Professor Maxon sailed with his daughter for a long ocean voyage, which he hoped would aid him in rapid recuperation, and permit him to forget the nightmare memory of those three horrible days and nights in his workshop.

He believed that he had reached an unalterable decision never again to meddle with the mighty, awe inspiring secrets of creation; but with returning health and balance he found himself viewing his recent triumph with feelings of renewed hope and anticipation.

The morbid fears superinduced by the shock following the sudden demise of the first creature of his experiments had given place to a growing desire to further prosecute his labors until enduring success had crowned his efforts with an achievement which he might exhibit with pride to the scientific world.

His recent disastrous success had convinced him that neither Ithaca or any other abode of civilization was a safe place to continue his experiments, but it was until their cruising had brought them among the multitudinous islands of the East Indies that the plan occurred to him that he finally adopted – a plan the outcome of which could he then have forseen would have sent him scurrying to the safety of his own country with the daughter who was to bear the full brunt of the horrors it entailed.

They were steaming up the China Sea when the idea first suggested itself, and as he sat idly during the long, hot days the thought grew upon him, expanding into a thousand wonderful possibilities, until it became crystalized into what was little short of an obsession.

The result was that at Manila, much to Virginia's surprise, he announced the abandonment of the balance of their purposed voyage, taking immediate return passage to Singapore. His daughter did not question him as to the cause of this change in plans, for since those three days that her father had kept himself locked in his workroom at home the girl had noticed a subtle change in her parent – a marked disinclination to share

8

with her his every confidence as had been his custom since the death of her mother.

While it grieved her immeasurably she was both too proud and too hurt to sue for a reestablishment of the old relations. On all topics other than his scientific work their interests were as mutual as formerly, but by what seemed a manner of tacit agreement this subject was taboo. And so it was that they came to Singapore without the girl having the slightest conception of her father's plans.

Here they spent nearly a month, during which time Professor Maxon was daily engaged in interviewing officials, English residents and a motley horde of Malays and Chinamen.

Virginia met socially several of the men with whom her father was engaged but it was only at the last moment that one of them let drop a hint of the purpose of the month's activity. When Virginia was present the conversation seemed always deftly guided from the subject of her father's immediate future, and she was not long in discerning that it was in no sense through accident that this was true. Thereafter her wounded pride made easy the task of those who seemed combined to keep her in ignorance.

It was a Dr. von Horn, who had been oftenest with her father, who gave her the first intimation of what was forthcoming. Afterward, in recollecting the conversation, it seemed to Virginia that the young man had been directed to break the news to her, that her father might be spared the ordeal. It was evident then that he expected opposition, but the girl was too loyal to let von Horn know if she felt other than in harmony with the proposal, and too proud to evince by surprise the fact that she was not wholly conversant with its every detail.

'You are glad to be leaving Singapore so soon?' he had asked, although he knew that she had not been advised that an early departure was planned.

'I am rather looking forward to it,' replied Virginia.

'And to a protracted residence on one of the Pamarung Islands?' continued von Horn.

'Why not?' was her rather non-committal reply, though she had not the remotest idea of their location.

Von Horn admired her nerve though he rather wished that she would ask some questions – it was difficult making progress in this way. How could he explain the plans when she evinced

9

not the slightest sign that she was not already entirely conversant with them?

'We doubt if the work will be completed under two or three years,' answered the doctor. 'That will be a long time in which to be isolated upon a savage little speck of land off the larger but no less savage Borneo. Do you think that your bravery is equal to the demands that will be made upon it?'

Virginia laughed, nor was there the slightest tremor in its note.

'I am equal to whatever fate my father is equal to,' she said, 'nor do I think that a life upon one of these beautiful little islands would be much of a hardship – certainly not if it will help to promote the success of his scientific experiments.'

She used the last words on a chance that she might have hit upon the true reason for the contemplated isolation from civilization. They had served their purpose too in deceiving von Horn who was now half convinced that Professor Maxon must have divulged more of their plans to his daughter than he had led the medical man to believe. Perceiving her advantage from the expression on the young man's face, Virginia followed it up in an endeavour to elicit the details.

The result of her effort was the knowledge that on the second day they were to sail for the Pamarung Islands upon a small schooner which her father had purchased, with a crew of Malays and lascars, and von Horn, who had served in the American navy, in command. The precise point of destination was still undecided – the plan being to search out a suitable location upon one of the many little islets which dot the western shore of Macassar Strait.

Of the many men Virginia had met during the month at Singapore von Horn had been by far the most interesting and companionable. Such time as he could find from the many duties which had devolved upon him in the matter of obtaining and outfitting the schooner, and signing her two mates and crew of fifteen, had been spent with his employer's daughter.

The girl was rather glad that he was to be a member of their little company, for she had found him a much travelled man and an interesting talker with none of the, to her, disgusting artificialities of the professional ladies' man. He talked to her as he might have talked to a man, of the things that interest intelligent people regardless of sex.

10

There was never any suggestion of familiarity in his manner; nor in his choice of topics did he ever ignore the fact that she was a young girl. She had felt entirely at ease in his society from the first evening that she had met him, and their acquaintance had grown to a very sensible friendship by the time of the departure of the Ithaca – the rechristened schooner which was to carry them away to an unguessed fate.

The voyage from Singapore to the Islands was without incident. Virginia took a keen delight in watching the Malays and lascars at their work, telling von Horn that she had to draw upon her imagination but little to picture herself a captive upon a pirate ship – the half naked men, the gaudy headdress, the earrings, and the fierce countenances of many of the crew furnishing only too realistically the necessary savage setting.

A week spent among the Pamarung Islands disclosed no suitable site for the professor's camp, nor was it until they had cruised up the coast several miles north of the equator and Cape Santang that they found a tiny island a few miles off the coast opposite the mouth of a small river – an island which fulfilled in every detail their requirements.

It was uninhabited, fertile and possessed a clear, sweet brook which had its source in a cold spring in the higher land at the island's center. Here it was that the Ithaca came to anchor in a little harbor, while her crew under von Horn, and the Malay first mate, Bududreen, accompanied Professor Maxon in search of a suitable location for a permanent camp.

The cook, a harmless old Chinaman called Sing Lee, and Virginia were left in sole possession of the Ithaca.

Two hours after the departure of the men into the jungle Virginia heard the fall of axes on timber and knew that the site of her future home had been chosen and the work of clearing begun. She sat musing on the strange freak which had prompted her father to bury them in this savage corner of the globe; and as she pondered there came a wistful expression to her eyes, and an unwonted sadness drooped the corners of her mouth.

Of a sudden she realized how wide had become the gulf between them now. So imperceptibly had it grown since those three horrid days in Ithaca just prior to their departure for what was to have been but a few months' cruise, that she had not until now comprehended that the old relations of open, good-fellowship had gone, possibly forever.

Had she needed proof of the truth of her sad discovery it had been enough to point to the single fact that her father had brought her here to this little island without making the slightest attempt to explain the nature of his expedition. She had gleaned enough from von Horn to understand that some important scientific experiments were to be undertaken; but what their nature was she could not imagine, for she had not the slightest conception of the success that had crowned her father's last experiment at Ithaca, although she had for years known of his keen interest in the subject.

The girl became aware also of other subtle changes in her father. He had long since ceased to be the jovial, carefree companion who had shared with her her every girlish joy and sorrow and in whom she had confided both the trivial and momentous secrets of her childhood. He had become not exactly morose, but rather moody and absorbed, so that she had of late never found an opportunity for the cozy chats that had formerly meant so much to them both. There had been too, recently, a strange lack of consideration for herself that had wounded her more than she had imagined. Today there had been a glaring example of it in his having left her alone upon the boat without a single European companion – something that he would never have thought of doing a few months before.

As she sat speculating on the strange change which had come over her father her eyes had wandered aimlessly along the harbor's entrance; the low reef that protected it from the sea, and the point of land to the south, that projected far out into the strait like a gigantic index finger pointing toward the mainland, the foliage covered heights of which were just visible above the western horizon.

Presently her attention was arrested by a tossing speck far out upon the rolling bosom of the strait. For some time the girl watched the object until at length it resolved itself into a boat moving head on toward the island. Later she saw that it was long and low, propelled by a single sail and many oars, and that it carried quite a company.

Thinking it but a native trading boat, so many of which ply the southern seas, Virginia viewed its approach with but idle

12

curiosity. When it had come to within half a mile of the anchorage of the Ithaca, and was about to enter the mouth of the harbor Sing Lee's eyes chanced to fall upon it. On the instant the old Chinaman was electrified into sudden and astounding action.

'Klick! Klick!' he cried, running toward Virginia. 'Go b'low, klick.'

'Why should I go below, Sing?' queried the girl, amazed by the demeanor of the cook.

'Klick! Klick!' he urged grasping her by the arm – half leading, half dragging her toward the companionway. 'Plilates! Mlalay plilates – Dlyak plilates.'

'Pirates!' gasped Virginia. 'Oh Sing, what can we do?'

'You go b'low. Mebbyso Sing flighten 'em. Shoot cannon. Bling help. Maxon come klick. Bling men. Chas'm 'way,' explained the Chinaman. 'But plilates see 'em pletty white girl,' he shrugged his shoulders and shook his head dubiously, 'then old Sing no can flighten 'em 'way.'

The girl shuddered, and crouching close behind Sing hurried below. A moment later she heard the boom of the old brass six pounder which for many years had graced the Ithaca's stern. In the bow Professor Maxon had mounted a modern machine gun, but this was quite beyond Sing's simple gunnery. The Chinaman had not taken the time to sight the ancient weapon carefully, but a gleeful smile lit his wrinkled, yellow face as he saw the splash of the ball where it struck the water almost at the side of the prahu.

Sing realized that the boat might contain friendly natives, but he had cruised these waters too many years to take chances. Better kill a hundred friends, he thought, than be captured by a single pirate.

At the shot the prahu slowed up, and a volley of musketry from her crew satisfied Sing that he had made no mistake in classifying her. Her fire fell short as did the ball from the small cannon mounted in her bow.

Virgina was watching the prahu from one of the cabin ports. She saw the momentary hesitation and confusion which followed Sing's first shot, and then to her dismay she saw the rowers bend to their oars again and the prahu move swiftly in the direction of the Ithaca.

It was apparent that the pirates had perceived the almost defenseless condition of the schooner. In a few minutes they would be swarming the deck, for poor old Sing would be entirely helpless to repel them. If Dr. von Horn were only there, thought the distracted girl. With the machine gun alone he might keep them off.

At the thought of the machine gun a sudden resolve gripped her. Why not man it herself? Von Horn had explained its mechanism to her in detail, and on one occasion had allowed her to operate it on the voyage from Singapore. With the thought came action. Running to the magazine she snatched up a feed-belt, and in another moment was on deck beside the astonished Sing.

The pirates were skimming rapidly across the smooth waters of the harbor, answering Sing's harmless shots with yells of derision and wild, savage war cries. There were, perhaps, fifty Dyaks and Malays – fierce, barbaric men; mostly naked to the waist, or with war-coats of brilliant colors. The savage head-dress of the Dyaks, the long, narrow, decorated shields, the flashing blades of parang and kris sent a shudder through the girl, so close they seemed beneath the schooner's side.

'What do? What do?' cried Sing in consternation. 'Go b'low, Klick!' But before he had finished his exhortation Virginia was racing toward the bow where the machine gun was mounted. Tearing the cover from it she swung the muzzle toward the pirate prahu, which by now was nearly within range above the vessel's side – a moment more and she would be too close to use the weapon upon the pirates.

Virginia was quick to perceive the necessity for haste, while the pirates at the same instant realized the menace of the new danger which confronted them. A score of muskets belched forth their missiles at the fearless girl behind the scant shield of the machine gun. Leaden pellets rained heavily upon her protection, or whizzed threateningly about her head – and then she got the gun into action.

At the rate of fifty a minute, a stream of projectiles tore into the bow of the prahu when suddenly a richly garbed Malay in the stern rose to his feet waving a white cloth upon the point of his kris. It was the Rajah Muda Saffir – he had seen the girl's face and at the sight of it the blood lust in his breast had been supplanted by another.

At sight of the emblem of peace Virginia ceased firing. She saw the tall Malay issue a few commands, the oarsmen bent to their work, the prahu came about, making off towards the harbor's entrance. At the same moment there was a shot from the shore followed by loud yelling, and the girl turned to see her father and von Horn pulling rapidly toward the Ithaca.

II

THE HEAVY CHEST

Virginia and Sing were compelled to narrate the adventure of the afternoon a dozen times. The Chinaman was at a loss to understand what had deterred the pirates at the very threshold of victory. Von Horn thought that they had seen the reinforcements embarking from the shore, but Sing explained that that was impossible since the Ithaca had been directly between them and the point at which the returning crew had entered the boats.

Virginia was positive that her fusillade had frightened them into a hasty retreat, but again Sing discouraged any such idea when he pointed to the fact that another instant would have carried the prahu close to the Ithaca's side and out of the machine gun's radius of action.

The old Chinaman was positive that the pirates had some ulterior motive for simulating defeat, and his long years of experience upon pirate infested waters gave weight to his opinion. The weak spot in his argument was his inability to suggest a reasonable motive. And so it was that for a long time they were left to futile conjecture as to the action that had saved them from a bloody encounter with these bloodthirsty sea wolves.

For a week the men were busy constructing the new camp, but never again was Virginia left without a sufficient guard for her protection. Von Horn was always needed at the work, for to him had fallen the entire direction of matters of importance that were at all of a practical nature. Professor Maxon wished to watch the building of the houses and the stockade, that he might offer such suggestions as he thought necessary, and again the girl noticed her father's comparative indifference to her welfare.

She had been shocked at his apathy at the time of the pirate attack, and chagrined that it should have been necessary for von Horn to have insisted upon a proper guard being left with her thereafter.

The nearer the approach of the time when he might enter

again upon those experiments which had now been neglected for the better part of a year the more self absorbed and moody became the professor. At times he was scarcely civil to those about him, and never now did he have a pleasant word or a caress for the daughter who had been his whole life but a few short months before.

It often seemed to Virginia when she caught her father's eyes upon her that there was a gleam of dislike in them, as though he would have been glad to have been rid of her that she might not in any way embarrass or interfere with his work.

The camp was at last completed, and on a Saturday afternoon all the heavier articles from the ship had been transported to it. On the following Monday the balance of the goods was to be sent on shore and the party were to transfer their residence to their new quarters.

Late Sunday afternoon a small native boat was seen rounding the point at the harbor's southern extremity, and after a few minutes it drew alongside the Ithaca. There were but three men in it – two Dyaks and a Malay. The latter was a tall, well built man of middle age, of a sullen and degraded countenance. His garmenture was that of the ordinary Malay boatman, but there was that in his mien and his attitude toward his companions which belied his lowly habiliments.

In answer to von Horn's hail the man asked if he might come aboard and trade; but once on the deck it developed that he had brought nothing wherewith to trade. He seemed not the slightest disconcerted by this discovery, stating that he would bring such articles as they wished when he had learned what their requirements were.

The ubiquitous Sing was on hand during the interview, but from his expressionless face none might guess what was passing through the tortuous channels of his Oriental mind. The Malay had been aboard nearly half an hour talking with von Horn when the mate, Bududreen, came on deck, and it was Sing alone who noted the quickly concealed flash of recognition which passed between the two Malays.

The Chinaman also saw the gleam that shot into the visitor's eye as Virginia emerged from the cabin, but by no word or voluntary outward sign did the man indicate that he had even noticed her. Shortly afterward he left, promising to return with

17

provisions the following day. But it was to be months before they again saw him.

That evening as Sing was serving Virginia's supper he asked her if she had recognized their visitor of the afternoon.

'Why no, Sing,' she replied, 'I never saw him before.'

'Sh!' admonished the celestial. 'No talkee so strong, wallee have ear all same labbit.'

'What do you mean, Sing?' asked the girl in a low voice. 'How perfectly weird and mysterious you are. Why, you make the cold chills run up my spine,' she ended, laughing. But Sing did not return her smile as was his custom.

'You no lememba tallee Lajah stand up wavee lite clothee in plilate boat, ah?' he urged.

'Oh, Sing,' she cried, 'I do indeed! But unless you had reminded me I should never have thought to connect him with our visitor of today – they do look very much alike, don't they?'

'Lookeelike! Ugh, they all samee one man. Sing know. You lookee out Linee,' which was the closest that Sing had ever been able to come to pronouncing Virginia.

'Why should I look out? He doesn't want me,' said the girl, laughingly.

'Don't you be too damee sure 'bout lat Linee,' was Sing's inelegant but convincing reply, as he turned toward his galley.

The following morning the party, with the exception of three Malays who were left to guard the Ithaca, set out for the new camp. The journey was up the bed of the small stream which emptied into the harbor, so that although fifteen men had passed back and forth through the jungle from the beach to the camp every day for two weeks, there was no sign that human foot had ever crossed the narrow strip of sand that lay between the dense foliage and the harbor.

The gravel bottom of the rivulet made fairly good walking, and as Virginia was borne in a litter between two powerful lascars it was not even necessary that she wet her feet in the ascent of the stream to the camp. The distance was short, the center of the camp being but a mile from the harbor, and less than half a mile from the opposite shore of the island which was but two miles at its greatest breadth, and two and a quarter at its greatest length.

At the camp Virginia found that a neat clearing had been

made upon a little tableland, a palisade built about it, and divided into three parts; the most northerly of which contained a small house for herself and her father, another for von Horn, and a common cook and eating house over which Sing was to preside.

The enclosure at the far end of the palisade was for the Malay and lascar crew and there also were quarters for Bududreen and the Malay second mate. The center enclosure contained Professor Maxon's workshop. This compartment of the enclosure Virginia was not invited to inspect, but as members of the crew carried in the two great chests which the professor had left upon the Ithaca until the last moment, Virginia caught a glimpse of the two buildings that had been erected within this central space – a small, square house which was quite evidently her father's laboratory, and a long, low thatched shed divided into several compartments, each containing a rude bunk. She wondered for whom they could be intended. Quarters for all the party had already been arranged for elsewhere, nor, thought she, would her father wish to house any in such close proximity to his workshop, where he would desire absolute quiet and freedom from interruption. The discovery perplexed her not a little, but so changed were her relations with her father that she would not question him upon this or any other subject.

As the two chests were being carried into the central campong, Sing, who was standing near Virginia, called her attention to the fact that Bududreen was one of those who staggered beneath the weight of the heavier burden.

'Bludleen, him mate. Why workee alsame lascar boy? Eh?' But Virginia could give no reason.

'I am afraid you don't like Bududreen, Sing,' she said. 'Has he ever harmed you in any way?'

'Him? No, him no hurt Sing. Sing poor,' with which more or less enigmatical rejoinder the Chinaman returned to his work. But he muttered much to himself the balance of the day, for Sing knew that a chest that strained four men in the carrying could contain but one thing, and he knew that Bududreen was as wise in such matters as he.

For a couple of months the life of the little hidden camp went on peacefully and without exciting incident. The Malay and lascar crew divided their time between watch duty on board the Ithaca, policing the camp, and cultivating a little patch of clearing just south of their own campong.

There was a small bay on the island's east coast, only a quarter of a mile from camp, in which oysters were found, and one of the Ithaca's boats was brought around to this side of the island for fishing. Bududreen often accompanied these expeditions, and on several occasions the lynx-eyed Sing had seen him returning to camp long after the others had retired for the night.

Professor Maxon scarcely ever left the central enclosure. For days and nights at a time Virginia never saw him, his meals being passed in to him by Sing through a small trap door that had been cut in the partition wall of the 'court of mystery' as von Horn had christened the section of the camp devoted to the professor's experimentations.

Von Horn himself was often with his employer as he enjoyed the latter's complete confidence, and owing to his early medical training was well fitted to act as a competent assistant; but he was often barred from the workshop, and at such times was much with Virginia.

The two took long walks through the untouched jungle, exploring their little island, and never failing to find some new and wonderful proof of Nature's creative power among its flora and fauna.

'What a marvellous thing is creation,' exclaimed Virginia as she and von Horn paused one day to admire a tropical bird of unusually brilliant plumage. 'How insignificant is man's greatest achievement beside the least of Nature's works.'

'And yet,' replied von Horn, 'man shall find Nature's secret some day. What a glorious accomplishment for him who first succeeds. Can you imagine a more glorious consummation of a man's life work – your father's, for example?'

The girl looked at von Horn closely.

'Dr. von Horn,' she said, 'pride has restrained me from asking what was evidently intended that I should not know. For years my father has been interested in an endeavor to solve the mystery of life – that he would ever attempt to utilize the secret should he have been so fortunate as to discover it had never occurred to me. I mean that he should try to usurp the functions of the Creator I could never have believed, but my knowledge of him, coupled with what you have said, and the extreme lengths to which he has gone to maintain absolute

20

secrecy for his present experiments can only lead to one inference; that his present work, if successful, would have results that would not be countenanced by civilized society or government. Am I right?'

Von Horn had attempted to sound the girl that he might, if possible, discover her attitude toward the work in which her father and he were engaged. He had succeeded beyond his hopes, for he had not intended that she should guess so much of the truth as she had. Should her interest in the work have proved favorable it had been his intention to acquaint her fully with the marvellous success which already had attended their experiments, and to explain their hopes and plans for the future, for he had seen how her father's attitude had hurt her and hoped to profit himself by reposing in her the trust and confidence that her father denied her.

And so it was that her direct question left him floundering in a sea of embarrassment, for to tell her the truth now would gain him no favor in her eyes, while it certainly would lay him open to the suspicion and distrust of her father should he learn of it.

'I cannot answer your question, Miss Maxon,' he said, finally, 'for your father's strictest injunction has been that I divulge to no one the slightest happening within the court of mystery. Remember that I am in your father's employ, and that no matter what my personal convictions may be regarding the work he has been doing I may only act with loyalty to his lightest command while I remain upon his payroll. That you are here,' he added, 'is my excuse for continuing my connection with certain things of which my conscience does not approve.'

The girl glanced at him quickly. She did not fully understand the motive for his final avowal, and a sudden intuition kept her from questioning him. She had learned to look upon von Horn as a very pleasant companion and a good friend – she was not quite certain that she would care for any change in their relations, but his remark had sowed the seed of a new thought in her mind as he had intended that it should.

When von Horn returned to the court of mystery he narrated to Professor Maxon the gist of his conversation with Virginia, wishing to forestall anything which the girl might say to her father that would give him an impression that von Horn had been talking more than he should. Professor Maxon listened to the narration in silence. When von Horn had finished, he cautioned him against divulging to Virginia anything that took place within the inner campong.

'She is only a child,' he said, 'and would not understand the importance of the work we are doing. All that she would be able to see is the immediate moral effect of these experiments upon the subjects themselves – she would not look into the future and appreciate the immense advantage to mankind that must accrue from a successful termination of our research. The future of the world will be assured when once we have demonstrated the possibility of the chemical production of a perfect race.'

'Number One, for example,' suggested von Horn.

Professor Maxon glanced at him sharply.

'Levity, Doctor, is entirely out of place in the contemplation of the magnificent work I have already accomplished,' said the professor tartly. 'I admit that Number One leaves much to be desired – much to be desired; but Number Two shows a marked advance along certain lines, and I am sure that tomorrow will divulge, in experiment Number Three, such strides as will forever silence any propensity toward scoffing which you may now entertain.'

'Forgive me, Professor,' von Horn hastened to urge. 'I did not intend to deride the wonderful discoveries which you have made, but it is only natural that we should both realize that Number One is not beautiful. To one another we may say what we would not think of suggesting to outsiders.'

Professor Maxon was mollified by this apology, and turned to resume his watch beside a large, coffin-shaped vat. For a while von Horn was silent. There was that upon his mind which he had wished to discuss with his employer since months ago, but the moment had never arrived which seemed at all propitious, nor did it appear likely ever to arrive. So the doctor decided to broach the subject now, as being psychologically as favorable a time as any.

'Your daughter is far from happy, Professor,' he said, 'nor do I feel that, surrounded as we are by semi-savage men, she is entirely safe.'

Professor Maxon looked up from his vigil by the vat, eyeing von Horn closely.

'Well?' he asked.

'It seemed to me that had I a closer relationship I might

better assist in adding to her happiness and safety – in short, Professor, I should like your permission to ask Virginia to marry me.'

There had been no indication in von Horn's attitude toward the girl that he loved her. That she was beautiful and intelligent could not be denied, and so it was small wonder that she might appeal strongly to any man, but von Horn was quite evidently not of the marrying type. For years he had roved the world in search of adventure and excitement. Just why he had left America and his high place in the navy he never had divulged; nor why it was that for seven years he had not set his foot upon ground which lay beneath the authority of Uncle Sam.

Sing Lee who stood just without the trap door through which he was about to pass Professor Maxon's evening meal to him could not be blamed for overhearing the conversation, though it may have been culpable in him in making no effort to divulge his presence, and possibly equally unpraiseworthy, as well as lacking in romance, to attribute the doctor's avowal to his knowledge of the heavy chest.

As Professor Maxon eyed the man before replying to his abrupt request, von Horn noted a strange and sudden light in the older man's eyes – something which he never before had seen there and which caused an uncomfortable sensation to creep over him – a manner of bristling that was akin neither to fear or horror, von Horn could not tell which.

Then the Professor arose from his seat and came very close to the younger man, until his face was only a few inches from von Horn's.

'Doctor,' he whispered in a strange, tense voice, 'you are mad. You do not know what you ask. Virginia is not for such as you. Tell me that she does not know of your feelings toward her. Tell me that she does not reciprocate your love. Tell me the truth man.' Professor Maxon seized von Horn roughly by both shoulders, his glittering eyes glaring terribly into the other's.

'I have never spoken to her of love, Professor,' replied von Horn quietly, 'nor do I know what her sentiments toward me may be. Nor do I understand, sir, what objections you may have to me – I am of a very old and noble family.' His tone was haughty but respectful.

23

Professor Maxon released his hold upon his assistant, breathing a sigh of relief.

'I am glad,' he said, 'that it has gone no further, for it must not be. I have other, nobler aspirations for my daughter. She must wed a perfect man – none such now exists. It remains for me to bring forth the ideal mate for her – nor is the time far distant. A few more weeks and we shall see such a being as I have long dreamed.' Again the queer light flickered for a moment in the once kindly and jovial eyes of the scientist.

Von Horn was horrified. He was a man of little sentiment. He could in cold blood have married this girl for the wealth he knew that she would inherit; but the thought that she was to be united with such a *thing* – 'Lord! It is horrible,' and his mind pictured the fearful atrocity which was known as Number One.

Without a word he turned and left the campong. A moment later Sing's knock aroused Professor Maxon from the reverie into which he had fallen, and he stepped to the trap door to receive his evening meal.

III

BEAUTY AND THE BEAST

One day, about two weeks later, von Horn and the professor were occupied closely with their work in the court of mystery. Developments were coming in riotous confusion. A recent startling discovery bade fare to simplify and expedite the work far beyond the fondest dreams of the scientist.

Von Horn's interest in the marvellous results that had been obtained was little short of the professor's – but he foresaw a very different outcome of it all, and by day never moved without a gun at either hip, and by night both of them were beside him.

Sing Lee, the noonday meal having been disposed of, set forth with rod, string and bait to snare gulls upon the beach. He moved quietly through the jungle, his sharp eyes and ears always alert for anything that might savor of the unusual, and so it was that he saw the two men upon the beach, while they did not see him at all.

They were Bududreen and the same tall Malay whom Sing had seen twice before – once in splendid raiment and commanding the pirate prahu, and again as a simple boatman come to the Ithaca to trade, but without the goods to carry out his professed intentions.

The two squatted on the beach at the edge of the jungle a short distance above the point at which Sing had been about to emerge when he discovered them, so that it was but the work of a moment or two for the Chinaman to creep stealthily through the dense underbrush to a point directly above them and not three yards from where they conversed in low tones – yet sufficiently loud that Sing missed not a word.

'I tell you, Bududreen, that it will be quite safe,' the tall Malay was saying. 'You yourself tell me that none knows of the whereabouts of these white men, and if they do not return your word will be accepted as to their fate. Your reward will be great if you bring the girl to me, and if you doubt the loyalty of any of your own people a kris will silence them as effectually as it will silence the white men.'

'It is not fear of the white men, oh, Rajah Muda Saffir, that deters me,' said Bududreen, 'but how shall I know that after I have come to your country with the girl I shall not myself be set upon and silenced with a golden kris – there be many that will be jealous of the great service I have done for the mighty rajah.'

Muda Saffir knew perfectly well that Bududreen had but diplomatically expressed a fear as to his own trustworthiness, but it did not anger him, since the charge was not a direct one; but what he did not know was of the heavy chest and Bududreen's desire to win the price of the girl and yet be able to save for himself a chance at the far greater fortune which he knew lay beneath that heavy oaken lid.

Both men had arisen now and were walking across the beach toward a small, native canoe in which Muda Saffir had come to the meeting place. They were out of earshot before either spoke again, so that what further passed between them Sing could not even guess, but he had heard enough to confirm the suspicions he had entertained for a long while.

He did not fish for gulls that day. Bududreen and Muda Saffir stood talking upon the beach, and the Chinaman did not dare venture forth for fear they might suspect that he had overheard them. If old Sing Lee knew his Malays, he was also wise enough to give them credit for knowing their Chinamen, so he waited quietly in hiding until Muda Saffir had left, and Bududreen returned to camp.

Professor Maxon and Von Horn were standing over one of the six vats that were arranged in two rows down the center of the laboratory. The professor had been more communicative and agreeable today than for some time past, and their conversation had assumed more of the familiarity that had marked it during the first month of their acquaintance at Singapore.

'And what of these first who are so imperfect?' asked von Horn. 'You cannot take them into civilization, nor would it be right to leave them here upon this island. What will you do with them?'

Professor Maxon pondered the question for a moment.

'I have given the matter but little thought,' he said at length.

'They are but the accidents of my great work. It is unfortunate that they are as they are, but without them I could have never reached the perfection that I am sure we are to find here,' and he tapped lovingly upon the heavy glass cover of the vat before which he stood. 'And this is but the beginning. There can be no more mistakes now, though I doubt if we can ever improve upon that which is so rapidly developing here.' Again he passed his long, slender hand caressingly over the coffin-like vat at the head of which was a placard bearing the words, NUMBER THIRTEEN.

'But the others, Professor!' insisted von Horn. 'We must decide. Already they have become a problem of no small dimensions. Yesterday Number Five desired some plantains that I had given to Number Seven. I tried to reason with him, but, as you know, he is mentally defective, and for answer he rushed at Number Seven to tear the coveted morsel from him. The result was a battle royal that might have put to shame two Bengal tigers. Twelve is tractable and intelligent. With his assistance and my bull whip I succeeded in separating them before either was killed. Your greatest error was in striving at first for such physical perfection. You have overdone it, with the result that the court of mystery is peopled by a dozen brutes of awful muscularity, and scarcely enough brain among the dozen to equip three properly.'

'They are as they are,' replied the professor. 'I shall do for them what I can – when I am gone they must look to themselves. I can see no way out of it.'

'What you have given you may take away,' said von Horn, in a low tone.

Professor Maxon shuddered. Those three horrid days in the workshop at Ithaca flooded his memory with all the gruesome details he had tried for so many months to forget. The haunting ghosts of the mental anguish that had left him an altered man – so altered that there were times when he had feared for his sanity!

'No, no!' he almost shouted. 'It would be murder. They are—'

'They are *things*,' interrupted von Horn. 'They are not human – they are not even beast. They are terrible, soulless creatures. You have no right to permit them to live longer than to substantiate your theory. None but us knows of their

27

existence – no other need know of their passing. It must be done. They are a constant and growing menace to us all, but most of all to your daughter.'

A cunning look came into the professor's eyes.

'I understand,' he said. 'The precedent once established, all must perish by its edict – even those which may not be grotesque or bestial – even this perfect one,' and he touched again the vat, 'and thus you would rid yourself of rival suitors. But no!' he went on in a high, trembling voice. 'I shall not be led to thus compromise myself, and be thwarted in my cherished plan. Be this one what he may he shall wed my daughter!'

The man had raised himself upon his toes as he reached his climax – his clenched hand was high above his head – his voice fairly thundered out the final sentence, and with the last word he brought his fist down upon the vat before him. In his eyes blazed the light of unchained madness.

Von Horn was a brave man, but he shuddered at the maniacal ferocity of the older man, and shrank back. The futility of argument was apparent, and he turned and left the workshop.

Sing Lee was late that night. In fact he did not return from his fruitless quest for gulls until well after dark, nor would he vouchsafe any explanation of the consequent lateness of supper. Nor could he be found shortly after the evening meal when Virginia sought him .

Not until the camp was wrapped in the quiet of slumber did Sing Lee return – stealthy and mysterious – to creep under cover of a moonless night to the door of the workshop. How he gained entrance only Sing Lee knows, but a moment later there was a muffled crash of broken glass within the laboratory, and the Chinaman had slipped out, relocked the door, and scurried to his nearby shack. But there was no occasion for his haste – no other ear than his had heard the sound within the workshop.

It was almost nine the following morning before Professor Maxon and von Horn entered the laboratory. Scarcely had the older man passed the doorway than he threw up his hands in horrified consternation. Vat Number Thirteen lay dashed to the floor – the glass cover was broken to a million pieces – a sticky, brownish substance covered the matting. Professor Maxon hid his face in his hands.

'God!' he cried. 'It is all ruined. Three more days would have—'

'Look!' cried von Horn. 'It is not too soon.'

Professor Maxon mustered courage to raise his eyes from his hands, and there he beheld, seated in a far corner of the room a handsome giant, physically perfect. The creature looked about him in a dazed, uncomprehending manner. A great question was writ large upon his intelligent countenance. Professor Maxon stepped forward and took him by the hand.

'Come,' he said, and led him toward a smaller room off the main workshop. The giant followed docilely, his eyes roving about the room – the pitiful questioning still upon his handsome features. Von Horn turned toward the campong.

Virginia, deserted by all, even the faithful Sing, who, cheated of his sport on the preceding day, had again gone to the beach to snare gulls, became restless of the enforced idleness and solitude. For a time she wandered about the little compound which had been reserved for the whites, but tiring of this she decided to extend her stroll beyond the palisade, a thing which she had never before done unless accompanied by von Horn – a thing both he and her father had cautioned her against.

'What danger can there be?' she thought. 'We know that the island is uninhabited by others than ourselves, and that there are no dangerous beasts. And, anyway, there is no one now who seems to care what becomes of me, unless – unless – I wonder if he does care. I wonder if I care whether or not he cares. Oh, dear, I wish I knew,' and as she soliloquized she wandered past the little clearing and into the jungle that lay behind the campong.

As von Horn and Professor Maxon talked together in the laboratory before the upsetting of vat Number Thirteen, a grotesque and horrible creature had slunk from the low shed at the opposite side of the campong until it had crouched at the flimsy door of the building in which the two men conversed. For a while it listened intently, but when von Horn urged the necessity for dispatching certain 'terrible soulless

29

creatures' an expression of intermingled fear and hatred convulsed the hideous features, and like a great grizzly it turned and lumbered awkwardly across the campong toward the easterly, or back wall of the enclosure.

Here it leaped futilely a half dozen times for the top of the palisade, and then trembling and chattering in rage it ran back and forth along the base of the obstacle, just as a wild beast in captivity paces angrily before the bars of its cage.

Finally it paused to look once more at the senseless wood that barred its escape, as though measuring the distance to the top. Then the eyes roamed about the campong to rest at last upon the slanting roof of the thatched shed which was its shelter. Presently a slow idea was born in the poor, malformed brain.

The creature approached the shed. He could just reach the saplings that formed the frame work of the roof. Like a huge sloth he drew himself to the roof of the structure. From here he could see beyond the palisade, and the wild freedom of the jungle called to him. He did not know what it was but in its leafy wall he perceived many breaks and openings that offered concealment from the creatures who were plotting to take his life.

Yet the wall was not fully six feet from him, and the top of it at least five feet above the top of the shed – those who had designed the campong had been careful to set this structure sufficiently far from the palisade to prevent its forming too easy an avenue of escape.

The creature glanced fearfully toward the workshop. He remembered the cruel bull whip that always followed each new experiment on his part that did not coincide with the desires of his master, and as he thought of von Horn a nasty gleam shot his mismated eyes.

He tried to reach across the distance between the roof and the palisade, and in the attempt lost his balance and nearly precipitated himself to the ground below. Cautiously he drew back, still looking about for some means to cross the chasm. One of the saplings of the roof, protruding beyond the palm leaf thatch, caught his attention. With a single wrench he tore it from its fastenings. Extending it toward the palisade he discovered that it just spanned the gap, but he dared not attempt to cross upon its single slender strand.

Quickly he ripped off half a dozen other poles from the roof, and laying them side by side, formed a safe and easy path to freedom. A moment more and he sat astride the top of the wall. Drawing the poles after him, he dropped them one by one to the ground outside the campong. Then he lowered himself to liberty.

Gathering the saplings under one huge arm he ran, lumberingly, into the jungle. He would not leave evidence of the havoc he had wrought; the fear of the bull whip was still strong upon him. The green foliage closed about him and the peaceful jungle gave no sign of the horrid brute that roamed its shadowed mazes.

As von Horn stepped into the campong his quick eye perceived the havoc that had been wrought with the roof at the east end of the shed. Quickly he crossed to the low structure. Within its compartments a number of deformed monsters squatted upon their haunches, or lay prone upon the native mats that covered the floor.

As the man entered they looked furtively at the bull whip which trailed from his right hand, and then glanced fearfully at one another as though questioning which was the malefactor on this occasion.

Von Horn ran his eyes over the hideous assemblage.

'Where is Number One?' he asked, directing his question toward a thing whose forehead gave greater promise of intelligence than any of his companions.

The one addressed shook his head.

Von Horn turned and made a circuit of the campong. There was no sign of the missing one and no indication of any other irregularity than the demolished portion of the roof. With an expression of mild concern upon his face he entered the workshop.

'Number One has escaped into the jungle, Professor,' he said.

Professor Maxon looked up in surprise, but before he had an opportunity to reply a woman's scream, shrill with horror, smote upon their startled ears.

Von Horn was the first to reach the campong of the whites. Professor Maxon was close behind him, and the faces of both were white with apprehension. The enclosure was deserted. Not even Sing was there. Without a word the two men sprang through the gateway and raced for the jungle in the direction from which that single, haunting cry had come.

Virginia Maxon, idling beneath the leafy shade of the tropical foliage, became presently aware that she had wandered farther from the campong than she had intended. The day was sultry, and the heat, even in the dense shade of the jungle, oppressive. Slowly she retraced her steps, her eyes upon the ground, her mind absorbed in sad consideration of her father's increased moodiness and eccentricity.

Possibly it was this very abstraction which deadened her senses to the near approach of another. At any rate the girl's first intimation that she was not alone came when she raised her eyes to look full into the horrid countenance of a fearsome monster which blocked her path toward camp.

The sudden shock brought a single involuntary scream from her lips. And who can wonder! The thing thrust so unexpectedly before her eyes was hideous in the extreme. A great mountain of deformed flesh clothed in dirty, white cotton pajamas! Its face was of the ashen hue of a fresh corpse, while the white hair and pink eyes denoted the absence of pigment; a characteristic of Albinos.

One eye was fully twice the diameter of the other, and an inch above the horizontal plane of its tiny mate. The nose was but a gaping orifice above a deformed and twisted mouth. The thing was chinless, and its small, foreheadless head surmounted its colossal body like a cannon ball on a hill top. One arm was at least twelve inches longer than its mate, which was itself long in proportion to the torso, while the legs, similarly mismated and terminating in huge, flat feet that protruded laterally, caused the thing to lurch fearfully from side to side as it lumbered toward the girl.

A sudden grimace lighted the frightful face as the grotesque eyes fell upon this new creature. Number One had never before seen a woman, but the sight of this one awoke in the unplumbed depths of his soulless breast a great desire to lay his hands upon her. She was very beautiful. Number One wished to have her for his very own; nor would it be a difficult matter, so fragile was she, to gather her up in those great, brute arms and carry her deep into the jungle far out of hearing of the bull-whip man and the cold, frowning one who was continually measuring and weighing Number One and his companions, the while he scrutinized them with those strange, glittering eyes that frightened one even more than the cruel lash of the bull whip.

Number One lurched forward, his arms outstretched toward the horror stricken girl. Virginia tried to cry out again – she tried to turn and run; but the horror of her impending fate and the terror that those awful features induced left her paralyzed and helpless.

The thing was almost upon her now. The mouth was wide in a hideous attempt to smile. The great hands would grasp her in another second – and then there was a sudden crashing of the underbrush behind her, a yellow, wrinkled face and a flying pig-tail shot past her, and the brave old Sing Lee grappled with the mighty monster that threatened her.

The battle was short – short and terrible. The valiant Chinaman sought the ashen throat of his antagonist, but his wiry, sinewy muscles were as reeds beneath the force of that inhuman power that opposed them. Holding the girl at arm's length in one hand, Number One tore the battling Chinaman from him with the other, and lifting him bodily above his head, hurled him stunned and bleeding against the bole of a giant buttress tree. Then lifting Virginia in his arms once more he dived into the impenetrable mazes of the jungle that lined the more open pathway between the beach and camp.

IV

A NEW FACE

As Professor Maxon and von Horn rushed from the workshop to their own campong, they neglected, in their haste, to lock the door between, and for the first time since the camp was completed it stood unlatched and ajar.

The professor had been engaged in taking careful measurements of the head of his latest experiment, the while he coached the young man in the first rudiments of spoken language, and now the subject of his labors found himself suddenly deserted and alone. He had not yet been without the four walls of the workshop, as the professor had wished to keep him from association with the grotesque results of his earlier experiments, and now a natural curiosity tempted him to approach the door through which his creator and the man with the bull whip had so suddenly disappeared.

He saw before him a great walled enclosure roofed by a lofty azure dome, and beyond the walls the tops of green trees swaying gently in the soft breezes. His nostrils tasted the incense of fresh earth and growing things. For the first time he felt the breath of Nature, free and unconfined, upon his brow.

He drew his giant frame to its full height and drank in the freedom and the sweetness of it all, filling his great lungs to their fullest; and with the first taste he learned to hate the close and stuffy confines of his prison.

His virgin mind was filled with wonder at the wealth of new impressions which surged to his brain through every sense. He longed for more, and the open gateway of the campong was a scarce needed invitation to pass to the wide world beyond. With the free and easy tread of utter unconsciousness of self, he passed across the enclosure and stepped out into the clearing which lay between the palisade and the jungle.

Ah, here was a still more beautiful world! The green leaves nodded to him, and at their invitation he came and the jungle reached out its million arms to embrace him. Now before him, behind, on either side there was naught but glorious green beauty shot with splashes of gorgeous color that made him gasp in wonderment.

Brilliant birds rose from amidst it all, skimming hither and thither above his head – he thought that the flowers and the birds were the same, and when he reached out and plucked a blossom, tenderly, he wondered that it did not flutter in his hand. On and on he walked, but slowly, for he must not miss a single sight in the strange and wonderful place; and then, of a sudden, the quiet beauty of the scene was harshly broken by the crashing of a monster through the underbrush.

Number Thirteen was standing in a little open place in the jungle when the discordant note first fell upon his ears, and as he turned his head in the direction of the sound he was startled at the hideous aspect of the thing which broke through the foliage before him.

What a horrid creature! But on the same instant his eyes fell upon another borne in the arms of the terrible one. This one was different – very different – soft and beautiful and white. He wondered what it all meant, for everything was strange and new to him; but when he saw the eyes of the lovely one upon him, and her arms outstretched toward him, though he did not understand the words upon her lips, he knew that she was in distress. Something told him that it was the ugly things that carried her that was the author of her suffering.

Virginia Maxon had been half unconscious from fright when she suddenly saw a white man, clothed in coarse, white, native pajamas, confronting her and the misshapen beast that was bearing her away to what frightful fate she could but conjecture.

At the sight of the man her voice returned with returning hope, and she reached her arms towards him, calling upon him to save her. Although he did not respond she thought that he understood for he sprang toward them before her appeal was scarce uttered.

As before, when Sing had threatened to filch his new possession from him, Number One held the girl with one hand while he met the attack of this new assailant with the other; but here was a very different metal than had succumbed to him before.

It is true that Number Thirteen knew nothing whatever of personal combat, but Number One had but little advantage of him in the matter of experience, while the former was equipped with great natural intelligence as well as steel muscles no whit less powerful than his deformed predecessor .

So it was that the awful giant found his single hand helpless to cope with the strength of his foeman, and in a brief instant felt powerful fingers clutching at his throat. Still reluctant to surrender his hold upon his prize, he beat futilely at the face of his enemy, but at last the agony of choking compelled him to drop the girl and grapple madly with the man who choked him with one hand and rained mighty and merciless blows upon his face and head with the other.

His captive sank to the ground, too weak from the effects of nervous shock to escape, and with horror-filled eyes watched the two who battled over her. She saw that her would-be rescuer was young and strong featured – all together a very fine specimen of manhood; and to her great wonderment it was soon apparent that he was no unequal match for the great mountain of muscle that he fought.

Both tore and struck and clawed and bit in the frenzy of mad, untutored strife, rolling about on the soft carpet of the jungle almost noiselessly except for their heavy breathing and an occasional beast-like snarl from Number One. For several minutes they fought thus until the younger man succeeded in getting both hands upon the throat of his adversary, and then, choking relentlessly, he raised the brute with him from the ground and rushed him fiercely backward against the stem of a tree. Again and again he hurled the monstrous thing upon the unyielding wood, until at last it hung helpless and inert in his clutches, then he cast it from him, and without another glance at it turned toward the girl.

Here was a problem indeed. Now that he had won her, what was he to do with her? He was but an adult child, with the brain and brawn of a man, and the ignorance and inexperience of the new-born. And so he acted as a child acts, in imitation of what it had seen others do. The brute had been carrying the lovely creature, therefore that must be the thing for him to do, and so he stooped and gathered Virginia Maxon in his great arms.

She tried to tell him that she could walk after a moment's rest, but it was soon evident that he did not understand her, as a puzzled expression came to his face and he did not put her down as she asked. Instead he stood irresolute for a time, and then moved slowly through the jungle. By chance his direction was toward the camp, and this fact so relieved the girl's mind that presently she was far from loath to remain quietly in his arms.

After a moment she gained courage to look up into his face. She thought that she never had seen so marvellously clean cut features, or a more high and noble countenance, and she wondered how it was that this white man was upon the island and she not have known it. Possibly he was a new arrival – his presence unguessed even by her father. That he was neither English nor American was evident from the fact that he could not understand her native tongue. Who could he be! What was he doing upon their island!

As she watched his face he suddenly turned his eyes down upon her, and as she looked hurriedly away she was furious with herself as she felt a crimson flush mantle her cheek. The man only half sensed, in a vague sort of way, the meaning of the tell tale color and the quickly averted eyes; but he became suddenly aware of the pressure of her delicate body against his, as he had not been before. Now he kept his eyes upon her face as he walked, and a new emotion filled his breast. He did not understand it, but it was very pleasant, and he knew that it was because of the radiant thing that he carried in his arms.

The scream that had startled von Horn and Professor Maxon led them along the trail toward the east coast of the island, and about halfway of the distance they stumbled upon the dazed and bloody Sing just as he was on the point of regaining consciousness.

'For God's sake Sing, what is the matter?' cried von Horn. 'Where is Miss Maxon?'

'Big blute, he catchem Linee. Tly kill Sing. Head hit tlee. No see any more. Wakee up – all glone,' moaned the Chinaman as he tried to gain his feet.

'Which way did he take her?' urged von Horn.

Sing's quick eyes scanned the surrounding jungle, and in a moment, staggering to his feet, he cried, 'Look see, klick! Foot plint!' and ran, weak and reeling drunkenly, along the broad trail made by the giant creature and its prey.

Von Horn and Professor Maxon followed closely in Sing's wake, the younger man horrified by the terrible possibilities

37

that obtruded themselves into his imagination despite his every effort to assure himself that no harm could come to Virginia Maxon before they reached her. The girl's father had not spoken since they discovered that she was missing from the campong, but his face was white and drawn; his eyes wide and glassy as those of one whose mind is on the verge of madness from a great nervous shock.

The trail of the creature was bewilderingly erratic. A dozen paces straight through the underbrush, then a sharp turn at right angles for no apparent reason, only to veer again suddenly in a new direction! Thus, turning and twisting, the tortuous way led them toward the south end of the island, until Sing, who was in advance, gave a sharp cry of surprise.

'Klick! Look see!' he cried excitedly. 'Blig blute dead — vely muchee dead.'

Von Horn rushed forward to where the Chinaman was leaning over the body of Number One. Sure enough, the great brute lay motionless, its horrid face even more hideous in death than in life, if it were possible. The face was black, the tongue protruded, the skin was bruised from the heavy fists of his assailant and the thick skull crushed and splintered from terrific impact with the tree.

Professor Maxon leaned over von Horn's shoulder. 'Ah, poor Number One,' he sighed, 'that you should have come to such an untimely end — my child, my child.'

Von Horn looked at him, a tinge of compassion in his rather hard face. It touched the man that his employer was at last shocked from the obsession of his work to a realization of the love and duty he owed his daughter; he thought that the professor's last words referred to Virginia.

'Though there are twelve more,' continued Professor Maxon, 'you were my first born son and I loved you most, dear child.'

The younger man was horrified.

'My God, Professor!' he cried. 'Are you mad? Can you call this thing "child" and mourn over it when you do not yet know the fate of your own daughter?'

Professor Maxon looked up sadly. 'You do not understand, Dr. von Horn,' he replied coldly, 'and you will oblige me, in the future, by not again referring to the offspring of my labors as "things".'

With an ugly look upon his face von Horn turned his back

upon the older man – what little feeling of loyalty and affection he had ever felt for him gone forever. Sing was looking about for evidence of the cause of Number One's death and the probable direction in which Virginia Maxon had disappeared.

'What on earth could have killed this enormous brute, Sing? Have you any idea?' asked von Horn.

The Chinaman shook his head.

'No savvy,' he replied. 'Blig flight. Look see,' and he pointed to the torn and trampled turf, the broken bushes, and to one or two small trees that had been snapped off by the impact of the two mighty bodies that had struggled back and forth about the little clearing.

'This way,' cried Sing presently, and started off once more into the brush, but this time in a northwesterly direction, toward camp.

In silence the three men followed the new trail, all puzzled beyond measure to account for the death of Number One at the hands of what must have been a creature of superhuman strength. What could it have been! It was impossible that any of the Malays or lascars could have done the thing, and there were no other creatures, brute or human, upon the island large enough to have coped even for an instant with the ferocious brutality of the dead monster, except – von Horn's brain came to a sudden halt at the thought. Could it be? There seemed no other explanation. Virginia Maxon had been rescued from one soulless monstrosity to fall into the hands of another equally irresponsible and terrifying.

Others then must have escaped from the campong. Von Horn loosened his guns in their holsters, and took a fresh grip upon his bull whip as he urged Sing forward upon the trail. He wondered which one it was, but not once did it occur to him that the latest result of Professor Maxon's experiments could be the rescuer of Virginia Maxon. In his mind he could see only the repulsive features of one of the others.

Quite unexpectedly they came upon the two, and with a shout von Horn leaped forward, his bull whip upraised. Number Thirteen turned in surprise at the cry, and sensing a new danger for her who lay in his arms, he set her gently upon the ground behind him and advanced to meet his assailant.

'Out of the way, you – monstrosity,' cried von Horn. 'If you

39

have harmed Miss Maxon I'll put a bullet in your heart!'

Number Thirteen did not understand the words that the other addressed to him but he interpreted the man's actions as menacing, not to himself, but to the creature he now considered his particular charge; and so he met the advancing man, more to keep him from the girl than to offer him bodily injury for he recognized him as one of the two who had greeted his first dawning consciousness.

Von Horn, possibly intentionally, misinterpreted the other's motive, and raising his bull whip struck Number Thirteen a vicious cut across the face, at the same time levelling his revolver point blank at the broad chest. But before ever he could pull the trigger an avalanche of muscle was upon him, and he went down to the rotting vegetation of the jungle with five sinewy fingers at his throat.

His revolver exploded harmlessly in the air, and then another hand wrenched it from him and hurled it far into the underbrush. Number Thirteen knew nothing of the danger of firearms, but the noise had startled him and his experience with the stinging cut of the bull whip convinced him that this other was some sort of instrument of torture of which it would be as well to deprive his antagonist.

Virginia Maxon looked on in horror as she realized that her rescuer was quickly choking Dr. von Horn to death. With a little cry she sprang to her feet and ran toward them, just as her father emerged from the underbrush through which he had been struggling in the trail of the agile Chinaman and von Horn. Placing her hand upon the great wrist of the giant she tried to drag his fingers from von Horn's throat, pleading meanwhile with both voice and eyes for the life of the man she thought loved her.

Again Number Thirteen translated the intent without understanding the words, and releasing von Horn permitted him to rise. With a bound he was upon his feet and at the same instant brought his other gun from his side pocket and levelled it upon the man who had released him; but as his finger tightened upon the trigger Virginia Maxon sprang between them and grasping von Horn's wrist deflected the muzzle of the gun just as the cartridge exploded. Simultaneously Professor Maxon sprang upon the doctor like a mad man, wrenching the revolver from his grasp and hurling him back with the superhuman strength of a maniac.

'Fool!' he cried. 'What would you do? Kill—,' and then of a sudden he realized his daughter's presence and the necessity for keeping the origin of the young giant from her knowledge.

'I am surprised at you, Dr. von Horn,' he continued in a more level voice. 'You must indeed have forgotten yourself to thus attack a stranger upon our island until you know whether he be friend or foe. Come! Escort my daughter to the camp, while I make the proper apologies to this gentleman.' As he saw that both Virginia and von Horn hesitated, he repeated his command in a peremptory tone, adding: 'Quick, now; do as I bid you.'

The moment had given von Horn an opportunity to regain his self-control, and realizing as well as did his employer, but from another motive, the necessity of keeping the truth from the girl, he took her arm and led her gently from the scene. At Professor Maxon's direction Sing accompanied them.

Now in Number Thirteen's brief career he had known no other authority than Professor Maxon's, and so it was that when his master laid a hand upon his wrist he remained beside him while another walked away with the lovely creature he had thought his very own.

Until after dark the professor kept the young man hidden in the jungle, and then, safe from detection, led him back to the laboratory.

V

TREASON

On their return to camp after her rescue Virginia talked a great deal to von Horn about the young giant who had rescued her, until the man feared that she was more interested in him than seemed good for his own plans.

He had now cast from him the last vestige of his loyalty for his employer, and thus freed had determined to use every means within his power to win Professor Maxon's daughter, and with her the heritage of wealth which he knew would be hers should her father, through some unforeseen mishap, meet death before he could return to civilization and alter his will, a contingency which von Horn knew he might have to consider should he marry the girl against her father's wishes, and thus thwart the crazed man's mad, but no less dear project.

He realized that first he must let the girl fully understand the grave peril in which she stood, and turn her hope of protection from her father to himself. He imagined that the initial step in undermining Virginia's confidence in her father would be to narrate every detail of the weird experiments which Professor Maxon had brought to such successful issues during their residence upon the island.

The girl's own questioning gave him the lead he needed.

'Where could that horrid creature have come from that set upon me in the jungle and nearly killed poor Sing?' she asked.

For a moment von Horn was silent, in well simulated hesitancy to reply to her query.

'I cannot tell you, Miss Maxon,' he said sadly, 'how much I should hate to be the one to ignore your father's commands, and enlighten you upon this and other subjects which lie nearer to your personal welfare than you can possibly guess, but I feel that after the horrors of this day duty demands that I must lay all before you – you cannot again be exposed to the horrors from which you were rescued only by a miracle.'

'I cannot imagine what you hint at, Dr. von Horn,' said Virginia, 'but if to explain to me will necessitate betraying my father's confidence I prefer that you remain silent.'

'You do not understand,' broke in the man, 'you cannot guess the horrors that I have seen upon this island, or the worse horrors that are to come. Could you dream of what lies in store for you you would seek death rather than face the future. I have been loyal to your father, Virginia, but were you not blind, or indifferent, you would long since have seen that your welfare means more to me than my loyalty to him – more to me than my life or my honor.

'You asked where the creature came from that attacked you today. I shall tell you. It is one of a dozen similarly hideous things that your father has created in his mad desire to solve the problem of life. He has solved it; but, God, at what a price in misshapen, soulless, hideous monsters!'

The girl looked up at him, horror stricken.

'Do you mean to say that my father in a mad attempt to usurp the functions of God created that awful thing?' she asked in a low, faint voice. 'And that there are others like it upon the island?'

'In the campong next to yours there are a dozen others,' replied von Horn, 'nor would it be easy to say which is the most hideous and repulsive. They are grotesque caricatures of humanity – without soul and almost without brain.'

'God!' murmured the girl, burying her face in her hands, 'he has gone mad; he has gone mad.'

'I truly believe that he is mad,' said von Horn, 'nor could you doubt it for a moment were I to tell you the worst.'

'The worst!' exclaimed the girl. 'What could be worse than that which you already have divulged? Oh, how could you have permitted it?'

'There is much worse than I have told you, Virginia. So much worse that I can scarce force my lips to frame the words, but you must be told. I would be more criminally liable than your father were I to keep it from you, for my brain, at least, is not crazed. Virginia, you have in your mind a picture of the hideous thing that carried you off into the jungle?'

'Yes,' and as the girl replied a convulsive shudder racked her frame.

Von Horn grasped her arm gently as he went on, as though

43

to support and protect her during the shock that he was about to administer.

'Virginia,' he said in a very low voice, 'it is your father's intention to wed you to one of his creatures.'

The girl broke from him with an angry cry.

'It is not true!' she exclaimed. 'It is not true. Oh, Dr. von Horn how could you tell me such a cruel and terrible untruth.'

'As God is my judge, Virginia,' and the man reverently uncovered as he spoke, 'it is the truth. Your father told me it in so many words when I asked his permission to pay court to you myself – you are to marry Number Thirteen when his education is complete.'

'I shall die first!' she cried.

'Why not accept me instead?' suggested the man.

For a moment Virginia looked straight into his eyes as though to read his inmost soul.

'Let me have time to considerd it, Doctor,' she replied. 'I do not know that I care for you in that way at all.'

'Think of Number Thirteen,' he suggested. 'It should not be difficult to decide .'

'I could not marry you simply to escape a worse fate,' replied the girl. 'I am not that cowardly – but let me think it over. There can be no immediate danger, I am sure.'

'One can never tell,' replied von Horn, 'what strange, new vagaries may enter a crazed mind to dictate this moment's action or the next.'

'Where could we wed?' asked Virginia.

'The Ithaca would bear us to Singapore, and when we returned you would be under my legal protection and safe.'

'I shall think about it from every angle,' she answered sadly, 'and now good night, my dear friend,' and with a wan smile she entered her quarters.

For the next month Professor Maxon was busy educating Number Thirteen. He found the young man intelligent far beyond his most sanguine hopes, so that the progress made was little short of uncanny.

Von Horn during this time continued to urge upon Virginia the necessity for a prompt and favorable decision in the matter of his proposal; but when it came time to face the issue squarely the girl found it impossible to accede to his request – she thought that she loved him, but somehow she dared not say the word that would make her his for life.

Bududreen, the Malay mate was equally harassed by conflicting desires, though of a different nature, for he had his eye upon the main chance that was represented to him by the great chest, and also upon the lesser reward which awaited him upon delivery of the girl to Rajah Muda Saffir. The fact that he could find no safe means for accomplishing both these ends simultaneously was all that had protected either from his machinations.

The presence of the uncanny creatures of the court of mystery had become known to the Malay and he used this knowledge as an argument to foment discord and mutiny in the ignorant and superstitious crew under his command. By boring a hole in the partition wall separating their campong from the inner one, he had disclosed to the horrified view of his men the fearsome brutes harbored so close to them. The mate, of course, had no suspicion of the true origin of these monsters, but his knowledge of the fact that they had not been upon the island when the Ithaca arrived and that it would have been impossible for them to have landed and reached the camp without having been seen by himself or some member of his company, was sufficient evidence to warrant him in attributing their presence to some supernatural and malignant power.

This explanation the crew embraced willingly, and with it Bududreen's suggestion that Professor Maxon had power to transform them all into similar atrocities. The ball once started gained size and momentum as it progressed. The professor's ofttimes strange expression was attributed to an evil eye, and every ailment suffered by any member of the crew was blamed upon their employer's Satanic influence. There was but one escape from the horrors of such a curse – the death of its author; and when Bududreen discovered that they had reached this point, and were even discussing the method of procedure, he added all that was needed to the dangerously smouldering embers of bloody mutiny by explaining that should anything happen to the white men he would become sole owner of their belongings, including the heavy chest, and that the reward of each member of the crew would be generous.

Von Horn was really the only stumbling block in Bududreen's path. With the natural cowardice of the Malay he feared this masterful American who never moved without a brace of guns slung about his hips; and it was at just this psychological moment that the doctor played into the hands of his subordinate, much to the latter's inward elation.

Von Horn had finally despaired of winning Virginia by peaceful court, and had about decided to resort to force when he was precipitantly confirmed in his decision by a conversation with the girl's father.

He and the professor were talking in the workshop of the remarkable progress of Number Thirteen toward a complete mastery of English and the ways of society, in which von Horn had been assisting his employer to train the young giant. The breach between the latter and von Horn had been patched over by Professor Maxon's explanations to Number Thirteen as soon as the young man was able to comprehend – in the meantime it had been necessary to keep von Horn out of the workshop except when the giant was confined in his own room off the larger one.

Von Horn had been particularly anxious, for the furtherance of certain plans he had in mind, to effect a reconciliation with Number Thirteen, to reach a basis of friendship with the young man, and had left no stone unturned to accomplish this result. To this end he had spent considerable time with Number Thirteen, coaching him in English and in the ethics of human association.

'He is progressing splendidly, Doctor,' Professor Maxon had said. 'It will be but a matter of a day or so when I can introduce him to Virginia, but we must be careful that she has no inkling of his origin until mutual affection has gained a sure foothold between them.'

'And if that should not occur?' questioned von Horn.

'I should prefer that they mated voluntarily,' replied the professor, the strange gleam leaping to his eyes at the suggestion of possible antagonism to his cherished plan, 'but if not, then they shall be compelled by the force of my authority – they both belong to me, body and soul.'

'You will wait for the final consummation of your desires until you return with them to civilization, I presume,' said von Horn.

'And why?' returned the professor. 'I can wed them here myself – it would be the surer way – yes, that is what I shall do.'

46

It was this determination on the part of Professor Maxon that decided von Horn to act at once. Further, it lent a reasonable justification for his purposed act.

Shortly after their talk the older man left the workshop, and von Horn took the opportunity to inaugurate the second move of his campaign. Number Thirteen was sitting near a window which let upon the inner court, busy with the rudiments of written English. Von Horn approached him.

'You are getting along nicely, Jack,' he said kindly, looking over the other's shoulder and using the name which had been adopted at his suggestion to lend a more human tone to their relations with the nameless man.

'Yes,' replied the other, looking up with a smile. 'Professor Maxon says that in another day or two I may come and live in his own house, and again meet his beautiful daughter. It seems almost too good to be true that I shall actually live under the same roof with her and see her every day – sit at the same table with her – and walk with her among the beautiful trees and flowers that witnessed our first meeting. I wonder if she will remember me. I wonder if she will be as glad to see me again as I shall be to see her.'

'Jack,' said von Horn, sadly, 'I am afraid there is a terrible and disappointing awakening for you. It grieves me that it should be so, but it seems only fair to tell you, what Professor Maxon either does not know or has forgotten, that his daughter will not look with pleasure upon you when she learns your origin.

'You are not as other men. You are but the accident of a laboratory experiment. You have no soul, and the soul is all that raises man above the beasts. Jack, poor boy, you are not a human being – you are not even a beast. The world, and Miss Maxon is of the world, will look upon you as a terrible creature to be shunned – a horrible monstrosity far lower in the scale of creation than the lowest order of brutes.

'Look,' and the man pointed through the window toward the group of hideous things that wandered aimlessly about the court of mystery. 'You are of the same breed as those, you differ from them only in the symmetry of your face and features, and the superior development of your brain. There is no place in the world for them, nor for you.

'I am sorry that it is so. I am sorry that I should have to be the one to tell you; but it is better that you know it now from a friend than that you meet the bitter truth when you least expected it, and possibly from the lips of one like Miss Maxon for whom you might have formed a hopeless affection.'

As von Horn spoke the expression on the young man's face became more and more hopeless, and when he had ceased he dropped his head into his open palms, sitting quiet and motionless as a carved statue. No sob shook his great frame, there was no outward indication of the terrible grief that racked him inwardly – only in the pose was utter dejection and hopelessness.

The older man could not repress a cold smile – it had had more effect than he had hoped.

'Don't take it too hard, my boy,' he continued. 'The world is wide. It would be easy to find a thousand places where your antecedents would be neither known nor questioned. You might be very happy elsewhere and there are a hundred thousand girls as beautiful and sweet as Virginia Maxon – remember that you have never seen another, so you can scarcely judge.'

'Why did he ever bring me into the world?' exclaimed the young man suddenly. 'It was wicked – wicked – terribly cruel and wicked.'

'I agree with you,' said von Horn quickly, seeing another possibility that would make his future plans immeasurably easier. 'It was wicked, and it is still more wicked to continue the work and bring still other unfortunate creatures into the world to be the butt and plaything of cruel fate.'

'He intends to do that?' asked the youth.

'Unless he is stopped,' replied von Horn.

'He must be stopped,' cried the other. 'Even if it were necessary to kill him.'

Von Horn was quite satisfied with the turn events had taken. He shrugged his shoulders and turned on his heel toward the outer campong.

'If he had wronged me as he has you, and those others,' with a gesture toward the court of mystery, 'I should not be long in reaching a decision.' And with that he passed out, leaving the door unlatched.

Von Horn went straight to the south campong and sought out Bududreen. Motioning the Malay to follow him they walked across the clearing and entered the jungle out of sight and hearing of the camp. Sing, hanging clothes in the north

48

end of the clearing saw them depart, and wondered a little.

'Bududreen,' said von Horn, when the two had reached a safe distance from the enclosures, 'there is no need of mincing matters – something must be done at once. I do not know how much you know of the work that Professor Maxon has been engaged in since we reached this island; but it has been hellish enough and it must go no further. You have seen the creatures in the campong next to yours?'

'I have seen,' replied Bududreen, with a shudder.

'Professor Maxon intends to wed one of these to his daughter,' von Horn continued. 'She loves me and we wish to escape – can I rely on you and your men to aid us? There is a chest in the workshop which we must take along too, and I can assure you that you all will be well rewarded for your work. We intend merely to leave Professor Maxon here with the creatures he has created.'

Bududreen could scarcely repress a smile – it was indeed too splendid to be true.

'It will be perilous work, Captain,' he answered. 'We should all be hanged were we caught.'

'There will be no danger of that, Bududreen, for there will be no one to divulge our secret.'

'There will be the Professor Maxon,' urged the Malay. 'Some day he will escape from the island, and then we shall all hang.'

'He will never escape,' replied von Horn, 'his own creatures will see to that. They are already commencing to realize the horrible crime he has committed against them, and when once they are fully aroused there will be no safety for any of us. If you wish to leave the island at all it will be best for you to accept my proposal and leave while your head yet remains upon your shoulders. Were we to suggest to the professor that he leave now he would not only refuse but he would take steps to make it impossible for any of us to leave, even to sinking the Ithaca. The man is mad – quite mad – Bududreen, and we cannot longer jeopardize our own throats merely to humor his crazy and criminal whims.'

The Malay was thinking fast, and could von Horn have guessed what thoughts raced through the tortuous channels of that semi-barbarous brain he would have wished himself safely housed in the American prison where he belonged.

49

'When do you wish to sail?' asked the Malay.

'Tonight,' replied von Horn, and together they matured their plans. An hour later the second mate with six men disappeared into the jungle toward the harbor. They, with the three on watch, were to get the vessel in readiness for immediate departure.

After the evening meal von Horn sat on the verandah with Virginia Maxon until the Professor came from the workshop to retire for the night. As he passed them he stopped for a word with von Horn, taking him aside out of the girl's hearing.

'Have you noticed anything peculiar in the actions of Thirteen?' asked the older man. 'He was sullen and morose this evening, and at times there was a strange, wild light in his eyes as he looked at me. Can it be possible that, after all, his brain is defective? It would be terrible. My work would have gone for naught, for I can see no way in which I can improve upon him.'

'I will go and have a talk with him later,' said von Horn, 'so if you hear us moving about in the workshop, or even out here in the campong think nothing of it. I may take him for a long walk. It is possible that the hard study and close confinement to that little building have been too severe upon his brain and nerves. A long walk each evening may bring him around all right.'

'Splendid – splendid,' replied the professor. 'You may be quite right. Do it by all means, my dear doctor,' and there was a touch of the old, friendly, sane tone which had been so long missing, that almost caused von Horn to feel a trace of compunction for the hideous act of disloyalty that he was on the very verge of perpetrating.

As Professor Maxon entered the house von Horn returned to Virginia and suggested that they take a short walk outside the campong before retiring. The girl readily acquiesced to the plan, and a moment later found them strolling through the clearing toward the southern end of the camp. In the dark shadows of the gateway leading to the men's enclosure a figure crouched. The girl did not see it, but as they came opposite it von Horn coughed twice, and then the two passed on toward the edge of the jungle.

VI

TO KILL!

The Rajah Muda Saffir tiring of the excuses and delays which Bududreen interposed to postpone the fulfilment of his agreement with the former, whereby he was to deliver into the hands of the rajah a certain beautiful maiden, decided at last to act upon his own initiative. The truth of the matter was that he had come to suspect the motives of the first mate of the Ithaca, and not knowing of the great chest attributed them to Bududreen's desire to possess the girl for himself.

So it was that as the second mate of the Ithaca with his six men waded down the bed of the little stream toward the harbor and the ship, a fleet of ten war prahus manned by over five hundred fierce Dyaks and commanded by Muda Saffir himself, pulled cautiously into the little cove upon the opposite side of the island, and landed but a quarter of a mile from camp.

At the same moment von Horn was leading Virginia Maxon farther and farther from the north campong where resistance, if there was to be any, would be most likely to occur. At his superior's cough Bududreen had signalled silently to the men within the enclosure, and a moment later six savage lascars crept stealthily to his side.

The moment that von Horn and the girl were entirely concealed by the darkness, the seven moved cautiously along the shadow of the palisade toward the north campong. There was murder in the cowardly hearts of several of them, and cupidity and lust in the hearts of all. There was no single one who would not betray his best friend for a handful of silver, nor any but was inwardly hoping and scheming to the end that he might alone possess both the chest and the girl.

It was such a pack of scoundrels that Bududreen led toward the north campong to bear away the treasure. In the breast of the leader was the hope that he had planted enough superstitious terror in their hearts to make the sight of the supposed author of their imagined wrongs sufficient provocation for his murder; for Bududreen was too sly to give the order for the killing of a white man – the arm of the white man's law was too long – but he felt that he would rest easier were he to leave the island with the knowledge that only a dead man remained behind with the secret of his perfidy.

While these events were transpiring Number Thirteen was pacing restlessly back and forth the length of the workshop. But a short time before he had had his author – the author of his misery – within the four walls of his prison, and yet he had not wreaked the vengeance that was in his heart. Twice he had been on the point of springing upon the man, but both times the other's eyes had met his and something which he was not able to comprehend had stayed him. Now that the other had gone and he was alone, contemplation of the hideous wrong that had been done him loosed again the flood gates of his pent rage.

The thought that he had been made by this man – made in the semblance of a human being, yet denied by the manner of his creation a place among the lowest of Nature's creatures – filled him with fury, but it was not this thought that drove him to the verge of madness. It was the knowledge, suggested by von Horn, that Virginia Maxon would look upon him in horror, as a grotesque and loathsome monstrosity.

He had no standard and no experience whereby he might classify his sentiments toward this wonderful creature. All he knew was that his life would be complete could he be near her always – see her and speak with her daily. He had thought of her almost constantly since those short, delicious moments that he had held her in his arms. Again and again he experienced in retrospection the exquisite thrill that had run through every fiber of his being at sight of her averted eyes and flushed face. And the more he let his mind dwell upon the wonderful happiness that was denied him because of his origin, the greater became his wrath against his creator.

It was now quite dark without. The door leading to Professor Maxon's campong, left unlatched earlier in the evening by von Horn for sinister motives of his own, was still unbarred through a fatal coincidence of forgetfulness on the part of the professor.

Number Thirteen approached this door. He laid his hand upon the knob. A moment later he was moving noiselessly across the campong toward the house in which Professor Maxon lay peacefully sleeping; while at the south gate Bududreen and his six cutthroats crept cautiously within and slunk in the dense shadows of the palisade toward the workshop where lay the heavy chest of their desire. At the same instant Muda Saffir with fifty of his head hunting Dyaks emerged from the jungle east of the camp, bent on discovering the whereabouts of the girl the Malay sought and bearing her away to his savage court far within the jungle fastness of his Bornean principality.

Number Thirteen reached the verandah of the house and peered through the window into the living room, where an oil lamp, turned low, dimly lighted the interior, which he saw was unoccupied. Going to the door he pushed it open and entered the apartment. All was still within. He listened intently for some slight sound which might lead him to the victim he sought, or warn him from the apartment of the girl or that of von Horn – his business was with Professor Maxon. He did not wish to disturb the others whom he believed to be sleeping somewhere within the structure – a low, rambling bungalow of eight rooms.

Cautiously he approached one of the four doors which opened from the living room. Gently he turned the knob and pushed the door ajar. The interior of the apartment beyond was in inky darkness, but Number Thirteen's greatest fear was that he might have stumbled upon the sleeping room of Virginia Maxon, and that if she were to discover him there, not only would she be frightened, but her cries would alarm the other inmates of the dwelling.

The thought of the horror that his presence would arouse within her, the knowledge that she would look upon him as a terrifying monstrosity, added new fuel to the fires of hate that raged in his bosom against the man who had created him. With clenched fists, and tight set jaws the great, soulless giant moved across the dark chamber with the stealthy noiselessness of a tiger. Feeling before him with hands and feet he made the circuit of the room before he reached the bed.

Scarce breathing he leaned over and groped across the covers with his fingers in search of his prey – the bed was empty. With the discovery came a sudden nervous reaction that sent him into a cold sweat. Weakly, he seated himself upon the edge of the bed. Had his fingers found the throat of Professor Maxon beneath the coverlet they would never have released their hold until life had forever left the body of the scientist, but now that the highest tide of the young man's hatred had come and gone he found himself for the first time assailed by doubts.

Suddenly he recalled the fact that the man whose life he sought was the father of the beautiful creature he adored. Perhaps she loved him and would be unhappy were he taken from her. Number Thirteen did not know, of course, but the idea obtruded itself, and had sufficient weight to cause him to remain seated upon the edge of the bed meditating upon the act he contemplated. He had by no means given up the idea of killing Professor Maxon, but now there were doubts and obstacles which had not been manifest before.

His standards of right and wrong were but half formed, from the brief attempts of Professor Maxon and von Horn to inculcate proper moral preceptions in a mind entirely devoid of hereditary inclinations toward either good or bad, but he realized one thing most perfectly – that to be a soulless thing was to be damned in the estimation of Virginia Maxon, and it now occurred to him that to kill her father would be the act of a soulless being. It was this thought more than another that caused him to pause in the pursuit of his revenge, since he knew that the act he contemplated would brand him the very thing he was, yet wished not to be.

At length, however, he slowly comprehended that no act of his would change the hideous fact of his origin; that nothing would make him acceptable in her eyes, and with a shake of his head he arose and stepped toward the living room to continue his search for the professor.

In the workshop Bududreen and his men had easily located the chest. Dragging it into the north campong the Malay was about to congratulate himself upon the ease with which the theft had been accomplished when one of his fellows declared his intention of going to the house for the purpose of dispatching Professor Maxon, lest the influence of his evil eye should overtake them with some terrible curse when the loss of the chest should be discovered.

While this met fully with Bududreen's plans he urged the man against any such act that he might have witnesses to prove that he not only had no hand in the crime, but had exerted his authority to prevent it; but when two of the men separated themselves from the party and crept toward the bungalow no force was interposed to stop them.

The moon had risen now, so that from the dark shadows of the palisade Muda Saffir and his savages watched the party with Bududreen squatting about the heavy chest, and saw the two who crept toward the house. To Muda Saffir's evil mind there was but one explanation. Bududreen had discovered a rich treasure, and having stolen that had dispatched two of his men to bring him the girl also.

Rajah Muda Saffir was furious. In subdued whispers he sent a half dozen of his Dyaks back beneath the shadow of the palisade to the opposite side of the bungalow where they were to enter the building, killing all within except the girl, whom they were to carry straight to the beach and the war prahus.

Then with the balance of his horde he crept along in the darkness until opposite Bududreen and the watchers about the chest. Just as the two who crept toward the bungalow reached it, Muda Saffir gave the word for the attack upon the Malays and lascars who guarded the treasure. With savage yells they dashed upon the unsuspecting men. Parangs and spears glistened in the moonlight. There was a brief and bloody encounter, for the cowardly Bududreen and his equally cowardly crew had no alternative but to fight, so suddenly had the foe fallen upon them.

In a moment the savage Borneo head hunters had added five grisly trophies to their record. Bududreen and another were racing madly toward the jungle beyond the campong.

As Number Thirteen arose to continue his search for Professor Maxon his quick ear caught the shuffling of bare feet upon the verandah. As he paused to listen there broke suddenly upon the still night the hideous war cries of the Dyaks, and the screams and shrieks of their frightened victims in the campong without. Almost simultaneously Professor Maxon and Sing rushed into the living room to ascertain the cause of the wild alarm, while at the same instant Bududreen's assassins sprang through the door with upraised krises, to be almost immediately followed by Muda Saffir's six Dyaks brandishing their long spears and wicked parangs.

In an instant the little room was filled with howling, fighting men. The Dyaks, whose orders as well as inclinations incited them to a general massacre, fell first upon Bududreen's lascars who, cornered in the small room, fought like demons for their lives, so that when the Dyaks had overcome them two of their own number lay dead beside the dead bodies of Bududreen's henchmen.

Sing and Professor Maxon stood in the doorway to the professor's room gazing upon the scene of carnage in surprise and consternation. The scientist was unarmed, but Sing held a long, wicked looking Colt in readiness for any contingency. It was evident that the celestial was no stranger to the use of his deadly weapon, nor to the moments of extreme and sudden peril which demanded its use, for he seemed no more perturbed than he had been but hanging out his weekly wash.

As Number Thirteen watched the two men from the dark shadows of the room in which he stood, he saw that both were calm – the Chinaman with the calmness of perfect courage, the other through lack of full understanding of the grave danger which menaced him. In the eyes of the latter shone a strange gleam – it was the wild light of insanity that the sudden nervous shock of the attack had brought to a premature culmination.

Now the four remaining Dyaks were advancing upon the two men. Sing levelled his revolver and fired at the foremost, and at the same instant Professor Maxon, with a shrill, maniacal scream, launched himself full upon a second. Number Thirteen saw the blood spurt from a superficial wound in the shoulder of the fellow who received Sing's bullet, but except for eliciting a howl of rage the missile had no immediate effect. Then Sing pulled the trigger again and again, but the cylinder would not revolve and the hammer fell futilely upon the empty cartridge. As two of the head hunters closed upon him the brave Chinaman clubbed his weapon and went down beneath them beating madly at the brown skulls.

The man with whom Professor Maxon had grappled had no opportunity to use his weapons for the crazed man held him close with one encircling arm while he tore and struck at him with his free hand. The fourth Dyak danced around the two with raised parang watching for an opening that he might deliver a silencing blow upon the white man's skull.

The great odds against the two men – their bravery in the face of death, their grave danger – and last and greatest, the fact that one was the father of the beautiful creature he worshipped, wrought a sudden change in Number Thirteen. In an instant he forgot that he had come here to kill the white-haired man, and with a bound stood in the center of the room – an unarmed giant towering above the battling four.

The parang of the Dyak who sought Professor Maxon's life was already falling as a mighty hand grasped the wrist of the head hunter; but even then it was too late to more than lessen the weight of the blow, and the sharp edge of the blade bit deep into the forehead of the white man. As he sank to his knees his other antagonist freed one arm from the embrace which had pinioned it to his side, but before he could deal the professor a blow with the short knife that up to now he had been unable to use, Number Thirteen had hurled his man across the room and was upon him who menaced the scientist.

Tearing him loose from his prey, he raised him far above his head and threw him heavily against the opposite wall, then he turned his attention towards Sing's assailants. All that had so far saved the Chinaman from death was the fact that the two savages were each so anxious to secure his head for the verandah rafters of his own particular longhouse that they interfered with one another in the consummation of their common desire.

Although battling for his life, Sing had not failed to note the advent of the strange young giant, nor the part he had played in succoring the professor, so that it was with a feeling of relief that he saw the newcomer turn his attention toward those who were rapidly reducing the citadel of his own existence.

The two Dyaks who sought the trophy which nature had set upon the Chinaman's shoulders were so busily engaged with their victim that they knew nothing of the presence of Number Thirteen until a mighty hand seized each by the neck and they were raised bodily from the floor, shaken viciously for an instant, and then hurled to the opposite end of the room upon the bodies of the two who had preceded them.

As Sing came to his feet he found Professor Maxon lying in a pool of his own blood, a great gash in his forehead. He saw the white giant standing silently looking down upon the old man. Across the room the four stunned Dyaks were recovering consciousness. Slowly and fearfully they regained their feet, and seeing that no attention was being paid them, cast a parting, terrified look at the mighty creature who had defeated them with his bare hands, and slunk quickly out into the darkness of the campong.

When they caught up with Rajah Muda Saffir near the beach, they narrated a fearful tale of fifty terrible white men with whom they had battled valiantly, killing many, before they had been compelled to retreat in the face of terrific odds. They swore that even then they had only returned because the girl was not in the house – otherwise they should have brought her to their beloved master as he had directed.

Now Muda Saffir believed nothing that they said, but he was well pleased with the great treasure which had so unexpectedly fallen into his hands, and he decided to make quite sure of that by transporting it to his own land – later he could return for the girl. So the ten war prahus of the Malay pulled quietly out of the little cove upon the east side of the island, and bending their way toward the south circled its southern extremity and bore away for Borneo.

In the bungalow within the north campong Sing and Number Thirteen had lifted Professor Maxon to his bed, and the Chinaman was engaged in bathing and bandaging the wound that had left the older man unconscious. The white giant stood beside him watching his every move. He was trying to understand why sometimes men killed one another and again defended and nursed. He was curious as to the cause of his own sudden change in sentiment toward Professor Maxon. At last he gave the problem up as beyond his powers of solution, and at Sing's command set about the task of helping to nurse the man whom he considered the author of his unhappiness and whom a few short minutes before he had come to kill.

As the two worked over the stricken man their ears were suddenly assailed by a wild commotion from the direction of the workshop. There were sounds of battering upon wood, loud growls and roars, mingled with weird shrieks and screams and the strange, uncanny gibbering of brainless things.

Sing looked quickly up at his companion.

'Whallee mallee?' he asked.

The giant did not answer. An expression of pain crossed his features, and he shuddered – but not from fear.

VII

THE BULL WHIP

As von Horn and Virginia Maxon walked slowly beneath the dense shadows of the jungle he again renewed his suit. It would please him more to have the girl accompany him voluntarily than to be compelled to take her by force, but take her he would one way or another, and that this very night, for all the plans were made and already under way.

'I cannot do it, Doctor von Horn,' she had said. 'No matter how much danger I may be in here I cannot desert my father on this lonely isle with only savage lascars and the terrible monsters of his own creation surrounding him. Why, it would be little short of murder for us to do such a thing. I cannot see how you, his most trusted lieutenant, can even give an instant's consideration to the idea.

'And now that you insist that his mind is sorely affected, it is only an added reason why I must remain with him to protect him so far as I am able, from himself and his enemies.'

Von Horn did not relish the insinuation in the accent which the girl put upon the last word.

'It is because I love you so, Virginia,' he hastened to urge in extenuation of his suggested disloyalty. 'I cannot see you sacrificed to his horrible mania. You do not realize the imminence of your peril. Tomorrow Number Thirteen was to have come to live beneath the same roof with you. You recall Number One whom the stranger killed as the thing was bearing you away through the jungle? Can you imagine sleeping in the same house with such a soulless thing? Eating your three meals a day at the same table with it? And knowing all the time that in a few short weeks at the most you were destined to be given to the thing as its mate? Virginia you must be mad to consider for a moment remaining within reach of such a terrible peril.

'Come to Singapore with me – it will take but a few days – and then we can return with some good medical man and a couple of Europeans, and take your father away from the terrible creatures he has created. You will be mine then and safe from the awful fate that now lies back there in the camp awaiting you. We can take your father upon a long trip where rest and quiet have an opportunity to restore his enfeebled mentality. Come, Virginia! Come with me now. We can go directly to the Ithaca and safety. Say that you will come.'

The girl shook her hread.

'I do not love you, I am afraid, Doctor von Horn, or I should certainly be moved by your appeal. If you wish to bring help for my father I shall never cease to thank you if you will go to Singapore to fetch it, but it is not necessary that I go. My place is here, near him.'

In the darkness the girl did not see the change that came over the man's face, but his next words revealed his altered attitude with sufficient exactitude to thoroughly arouse her fears.

'Virginia,' he said, 'I love you, and I intend to have you. Nothing on earth can prevent me. When you know me better you will return my love, but now I must risk offending you that I may save you for myself from the monstrous connection which your father contemplates for you. If you will not come away from the island with me voluntarily I consider it my duty to take you away by force.'

'You would never do that, Doctor von Horn!' she exclaimed.

Von Horn had gone too far. He cursed himself inwardly for a fool. Why the devil didn't that villain, Bududreen, come! He should have been along to act his part half an hour ago.

'No, Virginia,' said the man, softly, after a moment's silence, 'I could not do that; though my judgment tells me that I should do it. You shall remain here if you insist and I will be with you to serve and protect both you and your father.'

The words were fair, but the girl could not forget the ugly tone that had tinged his preceding statement. She felt that she would be glad when she found herself safely within the bungalow once more.

'Come,' she said, 'it is late. Let us return to camp.'

Von Horn was about to reply when the war cries of Muda Saffir's Dyaks as they rushed out upon Bududreen and his companions came to them distinctly through the tropic night.

'What was that?' cried the girl in an alarmed tone.

'God knows,' replied von Horn. 'Can it be that our men have mutinied?'

He thought the six with Bududreen were carrying out their part in a most realistic manner, and a grim smile tinged his hard face.

Virginia Maxon turned resolutely toward the camp.

'I must go back there to my father,' she said, 'and so must you. Our place is there – God give that we be not too late,' and before von Horn could stop her she turned and ran through the darkness of the jungle in the direction of the camp.

Von Horn dashed after her, but so black was the night beneath the overhanging trees, festooned with their dark myriad creepers, that the girl was out of sight in an instant, and upon the soft carpet of the rotting vegetation her light footfalls gave back no sound.

The doctor made straight for the camp, but Virginia, unused to jungle trailing even by day, veered sharply to the left. The sounds which had guided her at first soon died out, the brush became thicker, and presently she realized that she had no conception of the direction of the camp. Coming to a spot where the trees were less dense, and a little moonlight filtered to the ground, she paused to rest and attempt to regain her bearings.

As she stood listening for some sound which might indicate the whereabouts of the camp, she detected the noise of a body approaching through the underbrush. Whether man or beast she could but conjecture and so she stood with every nerve taut waiting the thing that floundered heavily toward her. She hoped it might be von Horn, but the hideous war cries which had appraised her of enemies at the encampment made her fear that fate might be directing the footsteps of one of these upon her.

Nearer and nearer came the sound, and the girl stood poised ready to fly when the dark face of Bududreen suddenly emerged into the moonlight beside her. With an hysterical cry of relief the girl greeted him.

'Oh, Bududreen,' she exclaimed, 'what has happened at camp? Where is my father? Is he safe? Tell me.'

The Malay could scarce believe the good fortune which had befallen him so quickly following the sore affliction of losing the treasure. His evil mind worked quickly, so that he grasped the full possibilities that were his before the girl had finished her questioning.

'The camp was attacked by Dyaks, Miss Maxon,' he replied. 'Many of our men were killed, but your father escaped and has gone to the ship. I have been searching for you and Doctor von Horn. Where is he?'

'He was with me but a moment ago. When we heard the cries at camp I hastened on to discover what calamity had befallen us – we became separated.'

'He will be safe,' said Bududreen, 'for two of my men are waiting to guide you and the doctor to the ship in case you returned to camp before I found you. Come, we will hasten on to the harbor. Your father will be worried if we are long delayed, and he is anxious to make sail and escape before the Dyaks discover the location of the Ithaca.'

The man's story seemed plausible enough to Virginia, although she could not repress a little pang of regret that her father had been willing to go on to the harbor before he knew her fate. However, she explained that by her belief that his mind was unbalanced through constant application to his weird obsession.

Without demur, then, she turned and accompanied the rascally Malay toward the harbor. At the bank of the little stream which led down to the Ithaca's berth the man lifted her to his shoulder and thus bore her the balance of the way to the beach. Here two of his men were awaiting him in one of the ship's boats, and without words they embarked and pulled for the vessel.

Once on board Virginia started immediately for her father's cabin. As she crossed the deck she noticed that the ship was ready to sail, and even as she descended the companionway she heard the rattle of the anchor chain about the capstan. She wondered if von Horn could be on board too. It seemed remarkable that all should have reached the Ithaca so quickly, and equally strange that none of her own people were on deck to welcome her, or to command the vessel.

To her chagrin she found her father's cabin empty, and a moment's hurried investigation disclosed the fact that von Horn's was unoccupied as well. Now her doubts turned quickly to fears, and with a little gasp of dismay at the grim possibilities which surged through her imagination she ran quickly to the companionway, but above her she saw that the hatch was down, and when she reached the top that it was fastened.

Futilely she beat upon the heavy planks with her delicate hands, calling aloud to Bududreen to release her, but there was no reply, and with the realization of the hopelessness of her position she dropped back to the deck, and returned to her stateroom. Here she locked and barricaded the door as best she could, and throwing herself upon the berth awaited in dry-eyed terror the next blow that fate held in store for her.

Shortly after von Horn became separated from Virginia he collided with the fleeing lascar who had escaped the parangs of Muda Saffir's head hunters at the same time as had Bududreen. So terror stricken was the fellow that he had thrown away his weapons in the panic of flight, which was all that saved von Horn from death at the hands of the fear crazed man. To him, in the extremity of his fright, every man was an enemy, and the doctor had a tough scuffle with him before he could impress upon the fellow that he was a friend.

From him von Horn obtained an incoherent account of the attack, together with the statement that he was the only person in camp that had escaped, all the others having been cut down by the savage horde that overwhelmed them. It was with difficulty that von Horn persuaded the man to return with him to the campong, but finally he consented to do so when the doctor with drawn revolver, presented death as the only alternative.

Together they cautiously crept back toward the palisade, not knowing at what moment they might come upon the savage enemy that had wrought such havoc among their forces, for von Horn believed the lascar's story that all had perished. His only motive for returning lay in his desire to prevent Virginia Maxon falling into the hands of the Dyaks, or, failing that, rescuing her from their clutches.

Whatever faults and vices were Carl von Horn's, cowardice was not one of them, and it was without an instant's hesitation that he had elected to return to succor the girl he believed to have returned to camp, although he entertained no scruples regarding the further pursuit of his dishonorable intentions toward her, should he succeed in saving her from her other enemies.

As the two approached the campong quiet seemed to have again fallen about the scene of the recent alarm. Muda Saffir had passed on toward the cove with the heavy chest, and the scrimmage in the bungalow was over. But von Horn did not abate his watchfulness as he stole silently within the precincts of the north campong, and, hugging the denser shadows of the palisade, crept toward the house.

The dim light in the living room drew him to one of the windows which overlooked the verandah. A glance within showed him Sing and Number Thirteen bending over the body of Professor Maxon. He noted the handsome face and perfect figure of the young giant. He saw the bodies of the dead lascars and Dyaks. Then he saw Sing and the young man lift Professor Maxon tenderly in their arms and bear him to his own room.

A sudden wave of jealous rage swept through the man's vicious brain. He saw that the soulless thing within was endowed with a kindlier and more noble nature than he himself possessed. He had planted the seed of hatred and revenge within his untutored heart without avail, for he read in the dead bodies of Bududreen's men and the two Dyaks the story of Number Thirteen's defence of the man von Horn had hoped he would kill.

Von Horn was quite sure now that Virginia Maxon was not within the campong. Either she had become confused and lost in the jungle after she left him, or had fallen into the hands of the wild horde that had attacked the camp. Convinced of this, there was no obstacle to thwart the sudden plan which entered his malign brain. With a single act he could rid himself of the man whom he had come to look upon as a rival, whose physical beauty aroused his envy and jealousy; he could remove, in the person of Professor Maxon, the parental obstacle which might either prevent his obtaining the girl, or make serious trouble for him in case he took her by force, and at the same time he could transfer to the girl's possession the fortune which was now her father's – and he could accomplish it all without tainting his own hands with the blood of his victims.

As the full possibilities of his devilish scheme unfolded before his mind's eye a grim smile curled his straight, thin lips at the thought of the fate which it entailed for the creator of the hideous monsters of the court of mystery.

As he turned away from the bungalow his eye fell upon the trembling lascar who had accompanied him to the edge of the verandah. He must be rid of the fellow in some way – no eye must see him perpetrate the deed he had in mind. A solution quickly occurred to him.

'Hasten to the harbor,' he said to the man in a low voice, 'and tell those on board the ship that I shall join them presently. Have all in readiness to sail. I wish to fetch some of my belongings – all within the bungalow are dead.'

No command could have better suited the sailor. Without a word he turned and fled toward the jungle. Von Horn walked quickly to the workshop. The door hung open. Through the dark interior he strode straight to the opposite door which let upon the court of mystery. On a nail driven into the door frame hung a heavy bull whip. The doctor took it down as he raised the strong bar which held the door. Then he stepped through into the moonlit inner campong – the bull whip in his right hand, a revolver in his left.

A half dozen misshapen monsters roved restlessly about the hard packed earth of the pen. The noise of the battle in the adjoining enclosure had aroused them from slumber and awakened in their half formed brains vague questionings and fears. At sight of von Horn several of them rushed for him with menacing growls, but a swift crack of the bull whip brought them to a sudden realization of the identity of the intruder, so that they slunk away, muttering and whining in rage.

Von Horn passed quickly to the low shed in which the remainder of the eleven were sleeping. With vicious cuts from the stinging lash he laid about him upon the sleeping things. Roaring and shrieking in pain and anger the creatures tumbled to their feet and lumbered awkwardly into the open. Two of them turned upon their tormentor, but the burning weapon on their ill protected flesh sent them staggering back out of reach, and in another moment all were huddled in the center of the campong.

As cattle are driven, von Horn drove the miserable creatures toward the door of the workshop. At the threshold of the dark interior the frightened things halted fearfully, and then as von Horn urged them on from behind with his cruel whip they milled as cattle at the entrance to a strange corral.

Again and again he urged them for the door, but each time they turned away, and to escape the whip beat and tore at the wall of the palisade in a vain effort to batter it from their path-

65

way. Their roars and shrieks were almost deafening as von Horn, losing what little remained of his scant self-control, dashed among them laying to right and left with the stern whip and the butt of his heavy revolver.

Most of the monsters scattered and turned back into the center of the enclosure, but three of them were forced through the doorway into the workshop, from the darkness of which they saw the patch of moonlight through the open door upon the opposite side. Toward this they scurried as von Horn turned back into the court of mystery for the others.

Three more herculean efforts he made before he beat the last of the creatures through the outer doorway of the workshop into the north campong.

Among the age old arts of the celestials none is more strangely inspiring than that of medicine. Odd herbs and unspeakable things when properly compounded under a favorable aspect of the heavenly bodies are potent to achieve miraculous cures, and few are the Chinamen who do not brew some special concoction of their own devising for the lesser ills which beset mankind.

Sing was no exception in this respect. In various queerly shaped, bamboo covered jars he maintained a supply of tonics, balms and lotions. His first thought when he had made Professor Maxon comfortable upon the couch was to fetch his pet nostrum, for there burned strong within his yellow breast the same powerful yearning to experiment that marks the greatest of the profession to whose mysteries he aspired.

Though the hideous noises from the inner campong rose threateningly, the imperturbable Sing left the bungalow and passed across the north campong to the little lean-to that he had built for himself against the palisade that separated the north enclosure from the court of mystery.

Here he rummaged about in the dark until he had found the two phials he sought. The noise of the monsters upon the opposite side of the palisade had now assumed the dimensions of pandemonium, and through it all the Chinaman heard the constant crack that was the sharp voice of the bull whip.

He had completed his search and was about to return to the bungalow when the first of the monsters emerged into the north campong from the workshop. At the door of his shack

Sing Lee drew back to watch, for he knew that behind them some one was driving these horribly grotesque creatures from their prison.

One by one they came lumbering into the moonlight until Sing had counted eleven, and then, after them, came a white man, bull whip and revolver in hand. It was von Horn. The equatorial moon shone full upon him – there could be no mistake. The Chinaman saw him turn and lock the workshop door; saw him cross the campong to the outer gate; saw him pass through toward the jungle, closing the gate.

Of a sudden there was a sad, low moaning through the surrounding trees; dense, black clouds obscured the radiant moon; and then with hideous thunder and vivid flashes of lightning the tempest broke in all its fury of lashing wind and hurtling deluge. It was the first great storm of the breaking up of the monsoon, and under the cover of its darkness Sing Lee scurried through the monster filled campong to the bungalow. Within he found the young man bathing Professor Maxon's head as he had directed him to do.

'All gettee out,' he said, jerking his thumb in the direction of the court of mystery. 'Eleven devils. Pletty soon come bung'low. What do?'

Number Thirteen had seen von Horn's extra bull whip hanging upon a peg in the living room. For answer he stepped into that room and took the weapon down. Then he returned to the professor's side.

Outside the frightened monsters groped through the blinding rain and darkness in search of shelter. Each vivid lightning flash, and bellowing of booming thunder brought responsive cries of rage and terror from their hideous lips. It was Number Twelve who first spied the dim light showing through the bungalow's living room window. With a low guttural to his companions he started toward the building. Up the low steps to the verandah they crept. Number Twelve peered through the window. He saw no one within, but there was warmth and dryness.

His little knowledge and lesser reasoning faculties suggested no thought of a doorway. With a blow he shattered the glass of the window. Then he forced his body through the narrow aperture. At the same moment a gust of wind sucking through the broken panes drew open the door, and as Number Thirteen, warned by the sound of breaking glass, sprang into the living room he was confronted by the entire horde of misshapen beings.

His heart went out in pity toward the miserable crew, but he knew that his life as well as those of the two men in the adjoining room depended upon the force and skill with which he might handle the grave crisis which confronted them. He had seen and talked with most of the creatures when from time to time they had been brought singly into the workshop that their creator might mitigate the wrong he had done by training the poor minds with which he had endowed them to reason intelligently.

A few were hopeless imbeciles, unable to comprehend more than the rudimentary requirements of filling their bellies when food was placed before them; yet even these were endowed with superhuman strength, and when aroused battled the more fiercely for the very reason of their brainlessness. Others, like Number Twelve, were of a higher order of intelligence. They spoke English, and, after a fashion, reasoned in a crude sort of way. These were by far the most dangerous, for as the power of comparison is the fundamental principle of reasoning, so they were able to compare their lot with that of the few other men they had seen, and with the help of von Horn to partially appreciate the horrible wrong that had been done them.

Von Horn, too, had let them know the identity of their creator, and thus implanted in their malformed brains the insidious poison of revenge. Envy and jealousy were there as well, and hatred of all beings other than themselves. They envied the ease and comparative beauty of the old professor and his assistant, and hated the latter for the cruelty of the bull whip and the constant menace of the ever ready revolver; and so as these were to them the representatives of the great human world of which they could never be a part, their envy and jealousy and hatred of these men embraced the entire race which they represented.

It was such that Number Thirteen faced as he emerged from the professor's apartment.

'What do you want here?' he said, addressing Number Twelve, who stood a little in advance of the others.

'We have come for Maxon,' growled the creature. 'We have been penned up long enough. We want to be out here. We have come to kill Maxon and you and all who have made us what we are.'

'Why do you wish to kill me?' asked the young man. 'I am one of you. I was made in the same way that you were made.'

Number Twelve opened his mismated eyes in astonishment.

'Then you have already killed Maxon?' he asked.

'No. He was wounded by a savage enemy. I have been helping to make him well again. He has wronged me as much as he has you. If I do not wish to kill him, why should you? He did not mean to wrong us. He thought that he was doing right. He is in trouble now and we should stay and protect him.'

'He lies,' suddenly shouted another of the horde. 'He is not one of us. Kill him! Kill him! Kill Maxon, too, and then we shall be as other men, for it is these men who keep us as we are.'

The fellow started forward toward Number Thirteen as he spoke, and moved by the impulse of imitation the others came on with him.

'I have spoken fairly to you,' said Number Thirteen in a low voice. 'If you cannot understand fairness here is something you can understand.'

Raising the bull whip above his head the young giant leaped among the advancing brutes and laid about him with mighty strokes that put to shame the comparatively feeble blows with which von Horn had been wont to deal out punishment to the poor, damned creatures of the court of mystery.

For a moment they stood valiantly before his attack, but after two had grappled with him and been hurled headlong to the floor they gave up and rushed incontinently out into the maelstrom of the screaming tempest.

In the doorway behind him Sing Lee had been standing waiting the outcome of the encounter and ready to lend a hand were it required. As the two men turned back into the professor's room they saw that the wounded man's eyes were open and upon them. At sight of Number Thirteen a questioning look came into his eyes.

'What has happened?' he asked feebly of Sing. 'Where is my daughter? Where is Dr. von Horn? What is this creature doing out of his pen?'

The blow of the parang upon the professor's skull had shocked his overwrought mind back into the path of sanity. It had left him with a clear remembrance of the past, other than the recent fight in the living room – that was a blank – and it had given him a clearer perspective of the plans he had been entertaining for so long relative to this soulless creature.

The first thought that sprung to his mind as he saw Number Thirteen before him was of his mad intention to give his daughter to such a monstrous thing. With the recollection came a sudden loathing and hatred of this and the other creatures of his unholy experimentations.

Presently he realized that his questions had not been answered.

'Sing!' he shouted. 'Answer me. Where are Virginia and Dr. von Horn?'

'All gonee. Me no know. All gonee. Maybeso allee dead.'

'My God!' groaned the stricken man; and then his eyes again falling upon the silent giant in the doorway, 'Out of my sight,' he shrieked. 'Out of my sight; Never let me see you again – and to think that I would have given my only daughter to a soulless thing like you. Away! Before I go mad and slay you.'

Slowly the color mounted to the neck and face of the giant – then suddenly it receded, leaving him as ashen as death. His great hand gripped the stock of the bull whip. A single blow was all that would have been needed to silence Professor Maxon forever. There was murder in the wounded heart. The man took a step forward into the room, and then something drew his eyes to a spot upon the wall just above Professor Maxon's shoulder – it was a photograph of Virginia Maxon.

Without a word Number Thirteen turned upon his heel and passed out into the storm.

VIII

THE SOUL OF NUMBER 13

Scarcely had the Ithaca cleared the reef which lies almost across the mouth of the little harbor where she had been moored for so many months than the tempest broke upon her in all its terrific fury. Bududreen was no mean sailor, but he was short handed, nor is it reasonable to suppose that even with a full crew he could have weathered the terrific gale which beat down upon the hapless vessel. Buffeted by great waves, and stripped of every shred of canvas by the force of the mighty wind that howled about her, the Ithaca drifted a hopeless wreck soon after the storm struck her.

Below deck the terrified girl clung desperately to a stanchion as the stricken ship lunged sickeningly before the hurricane. For half an hour the awful suspense endured, and then with a terrific crash the vessel struck, shivering and trembling from stem to stern.

Virginia Maxon sunk to her knees in prayer, for this she thought must surely be the end. On deck Bududreen and his crew had lashed themselves to the masts, and as the Ithaca struck the reef before the harbor, back upon which she had been driven, the tall poles with their living freight snapped at the deck and went overboard carrying every thing with them amid shrieks and cries of terror that were drowned and choked by the wild tumult of the night.

Twice the girl felt the ship strike upon the reef, then a great wave caught and carried her high into the air, dropping her with a nauseating lunge which seemed to the imprisoned girl to be carrying the ship to the very bottom of the ocean. With closed eyes she clung in silent prayer beside her berth waiting for the moment that would bring the engulfing waters and oblivion – praying that the end might come speedily and release her from the torture of nervous apprehension that had terrorized her for what seemed an eternity.

After the last, long dive, the Ithaca righted herself laboriously, wallowing drunkenly, but apparently upon an even keel in less turbulent waters. One long minute dragged after another, yet no suffocating deluge poured in upon the girl, and presently she realized that the ship had, at least temporarily, weathered the awful buffeting of the savage elements. Now she felt a gentle roll, though the wild turmoil of the storm still came to her ears through the heavy planking of the Ithaca's hull.

For a long hour she lay wondering what fate had overtaken the vessel and whither she had been driven, and then, with a gentle grinding sound, the ship stopped, swung around, and finally came to rest with a slight list to starboard. The wind howled about her, the torrential rain beat loudly upon her, but except for a slight rocking the ship lay quiet.

Hours passed with no other sounds than those of the rapidly waning tempest. The girl heard no signs of life upon the ship. Her curiosity became more and more keenly aroused. She had that indefinable, intuitive feeling that she was utterly alone upon the vessel, and at length, unable to endure the inaction and uncertainty longer, made her way to the companion ladder where for half an hour she futilely attempted to remove the hatch.

As she worked she failed to hear the scraping of naked bodies clambering over the ship's side, or the padding of unshod feet upon the deck above her. She was about to give up her work at the hatch when the heavy wooden cover suddenly commenced to move above her as though actuated by some supernatural power. Fascinated, the girl stood gazing in wide-eyed astonishment as one end of the hatch rose higher and higher until a little patch of blue sky revealed the fact that morning had come. Then the cover slid suddenly back and Virginia Maxon found herself looking into a savage and terrible face.

The dark skin was creased in fierce wrinkles about the eyes and mouth. Gleaming tiger cat's teeth curved upward from holes pierced to receive them in the upper half of each ear. The slit ear lobes supported heavy rings whose weight had stretched the skin until the long loop rested upon the brown shoulders. The filed and blackened teeth behind the loose lips added the last touch of hideousness to this terrible countenance.

Nor was this all. A score of equally ferocious faces peered down from behind the foremost. With a little scream Virginia

Maxon sprang back to the lower deck and ran toward her stateroom. Behind her she heard the commotion of many men descending the companionway.

As Number Thirteen came into the campong after quitting the bungalow his heart was a chaos of conflicting emotions. His little world had been wiped out. His creator – the man whom he thought his only friend and benefactor – had suddenly turned against him. The beautiful creature he worshipped was either lost or dead; Sing had said so. He was nothing but a miserable *thing*. There was no place in the world for him, and even should he again find Virginia Maxon he had von Horn's word for it that she would shrink from him and loathe him even more than another.

With no plans and no hopes he walked aimlessly through the blinding rain, oblivious of it and of the vivid lightning and deafening thunder. The palisade at length brought him to a sudden stop. Mechanically he squatted on his haunches with his back against it, and there, in the midst of the fury of the storm he conquered the tempest that raged in his own breast. The murder that rose again and again in his untaught heart he forced back by thoughts of the sweet pure face of the girl whose image he had set up in the inner temple of his being, as a gentle, guiding divinity.

'He made me without a soul,' he repeated over and over again to himself, 'but I have found a soul – she shall be my soul. Von Horn could not explain to me what a soul is. He does not know. None of them knows. I am wiser than all the rest, for I have learned what a soul is. Eyes cannot see it – fingers cannot feel it, but he who possesses it knows that it is there for it fills his whole breast with a great, wonderful love and worship for something infinitely finer than man's dull senses can gauge – something that guides him into paths far above the plain of soulless beasts and bestial men.

'Let those who will say that I have no soul, for I am satisfied with the soul that I have found. It would never permit me to inflict on others the terrible wrong that Professor Maxon has inflicted on me – yet he never doubts his own possession of a soul. It would not allow me to revel in the coarse brutalities of von Horn – and I am sure that von Horn thinks he has a soul. And if the savage men who came tonight to kill have souls,

73

then I am glad that my soul is after my own choosing – I would not care for one like theirs.'

The sudden equatorial dawn found the man still musing. The storm had ceased and as the daylight brought the surroundings to view Number Thirteen became aware that he was not alone in the campong. All about him lay the eleven terrible men who he had driven from the bungalow the previous night. The sight of them brought a realization of new responsibilities. To leave them here in the campong would mean the immediate death of Professor Maxon and the Chinaman. To turn them into the jungle might mean a similar fate for Virginia Maxon were she wandering about in search of the encampment – Number Thirteen could not believe that she was dead. It seemed too monstrous to believe that he should never see her again, and he knew so little of death that it was impossible for him to realize that that beautiful creature ever could cease to be filled with the vivacity of life.

The young man had determined to leave the camp himself – partly on account of the cruel words Professor Maxon had hurled at him the night before, but principally in order that he might search for the lost girl. Of course he had not the remotest idea where to look for her, but as von Horn had explained that they were upon a small island he felt reasonably sure that he should find her in time.

As he looked at the sleeping monsters near him he determined that the only solution of his problem was to take them all with him. Number Twelve lay closest to him, and stepping to his side, he nudged him with the butt of the bull whip he still carried. The creature opened his dull eyes.

'Get up,' said Number Thirteen.

Number Twelve rose, looking askance at the bull whip.

'We are not wanted here,' said Number Thirteen. 'I am going away and you are all going with me. We shall find a place where we may live in peace and freedom. Are you not tired of always being penned up?'

'Yes,' replied Number Twelve, still looking at the whip.

'You need not fear the whip,' said the young man. 'I shall not use it on those who make no trouble. Wake the others and tell them what I have said. All must come with me – those who refuse shall feel the whip.'

Number Twelve did as he was bid. The creatures mumbled

among themselves for a few minutes. Finally Number Thirteen cracked his long whip to attract their attention.

'Come!' he said.

Nine of them shuffled after him as he turned toward the outer gate – only Number Ten and Number Three held back. The young man walked quickly to where they stood eyeing him sullenly. The others halted to watch – ready to spring upon their new master should the tide of the impending battle turn against him. The two mutineers backed away snarling, their hideous features distorted in rage.

'Come!' repeated Number Thirteen.

'We will stay here,' growled Number Ten. 'We have not yet finished with Maxon.'

A loop in the butt of the bull whip was about the young man's wrist. Dropping the weapon from his hand it still dangled by the loop. At the same instant he launched himself at the throat of Number Ten, for he realized that a decisive victory now without the aid of the weapon they all feared would make the balance of his work easier.

The brute met the charge with lowered head and outstretched hands, and in another second they were locked in a clinch, tearing at one another like two great gorillas. For a moment Number Three stood watching the battle, and then he too sprang in to aid his fellow mutineer. Number Thirteen was striking heavy blows with his giant hands upon the face and head of his antagonist, while the long, uneven fangs of the latter had found his breast and neck a half dozen times. Blood covered them both. Number Three threw his enormous weight into the conflict with the frenzy of a mad bull.

Again and again he got a hold upon the young giant's throat only to be shaken loose by the mighty muscles. The excitement of the conflict was telling upon the malformed minds of the spectators. Presently one who was almost brainless, acting upon the impulse of suggestion, leaped in among the fighters, striking and biting at Number Thirteen. It was all that was needed – another second found the whole monstrous crew upon the single man.

His mighty strength availed him but little in the unequal conflict – eleven to one were too great odds even for those powerful thews. His great advantage lay in his superior intelligence, but even this seemed futile in the face of the enormous weight of numbers that opposed him. Time and again he had almost shaken himself free only to fall once more – dragged down by hairy arms about his legs.

Hither and thither about the campong the battle raged until the fighting mass rolled against the palisade, and here, at last, with his back to the structure, Number Thirteen regained his feet, and with the heavy stock of the bull whip beat off, for a moment, those nearest him. All were winded, but when those who were left of the eleven original antagonists drew back to regain their breath, the young giant gave them no respite, but leaped among them with the long lash they had such good reason to hate and fear.

The result was as his higher intelligence had foreseen – the creatures scattered to escape the fury of the lash and a moment later he had them at his mercy. About the campong lay four who had felt the full force of his heavy fist, while not one but bore some mark of the battle.

Not a moment did he give them to recuperate after he had scattered them before he rounded them up once more near the outer gate – but now they were docile and submissive. In pairs he ordered them to lift their unconscious comrades to their shoulders and bear them into the jungle, for Number Thirteen was setting out into the world with his grim tribe in search of his lady love.

Once well within the jungle they halted to eat of the more familiar fruit which had always formed the greater bulk of their sustenance. Thus refreshed, they set out once more after the leader who wandered aimlessly beneath the shade of the tall jungle trees amidst the gorgeous tropic blooms and gay, song-less birds – and of the twelve only the leader saw the beauties that surrounded them or felt the strange, mysterious influence of the untracked world they trod. Chance took them toward the west until presently they emerged upon the harbor's edge, where from the matted jungle they overlooked for the first time the waters of the little bay and the broader expanse of strait beyond, until their eyes rested at last upon the blurred lines of distant Borneo.

From other vantage points at the jungle's border two other watchers looked out upon the scene. One was the lascar whom von Horn had sent down to the Ithaca the night before but who had reached the harbor after she sailed. The other was von

Horn himself. And both were looking out upon the dismantled wreck of the Ithaca where it lay in the sand near the harbor's southern edge. Neither ventured forth from his place of concealment, for beyond the Ithaca ten prahus were pulling gracefully into the quiet waters of the basin.

Rajah Muda Saffir, caught by the tornado the preceding night as he had been about to beat across to Borneo, had scurried for shelter within one of the many tiny coves which indent the island's entire coast. It happened that his haven of refuge was but a short distance south of the harbor in which he knew the Ithaca to be moored, and in the morning he decided to pay that vessel a visit in the hope that he might learn something of advantage about the girl from one of her lascar crew.

The wily Malay had long refrained from pillaging the Ithaca for fear such an act might militate against the larger villainy he purposed perpetrating against her white owner, but when he rounded the point and came in sight of the stranded wreck he put all such thoughts from him and made straight for the helpless hulk to glean whatever of salvage might yet remain within her battered hull.

The old rascal had little thought of the priceless treasure hidden beneath the Ithaca's clean swept deck as he ordered his savage henchmen up her sides while he lay back upon his sleeping mat beneath the canopy which protected his vice-regal head from the blistering tropic sun.

Number Thirteen watched the wild head hunters with keenest interest as they clambered aboard the vessel. With von Horn he saw the evident amazement which followed the opening of the hatch, though neither guessed its cause. He saw the haste with which half a dozen of the warriors leaped down the companionway and heard their savage shouts as they pursued their quarry within the bowels of the ship.

A few minutes later they emerged dragging a woman with them. Von Horn and Number Thirteen recognized the girl simultaneously, but the doctor, though he ground his teeth in futile rage, knew that he was helpless to avert the tragedy. Number Thirteen neither knew nor cared.

'Come!' he called to his grotesque horde. 'Kill the men and save the girl – the one with the golden hair,' he added as the sudden realization came to him that none of these creatures ever had seen a woman before. Then he dashed from the shelter of the jungle, across the beach and into the water, his fearful pack at his heels.

The Ithaca lay now in about five feet of water, and the war prahus of Muda Saffir rode upon her seaward side, so that those who manned them did not see the twelve who splashed through the water from land. Never before had any of the rescuers seen a larger body of water than the little stream which wound through their campong, but accidents and experiments in that had taught them the danger of submerging their heads. They could not swim, but all were large and strong, so that they were able to push their way rapidly through the water to the very side of the ship.

Here they found difficulty in reaching the deck, but in a moment Number Thirteen had solved the problem by requiring one of the taller of his crew to stand close in by the ship while the others clambered upon his shoulders and from there to the Ithaca's deck.

Number Thirteen was the first to pull himself over the vessel's side, and as he did so he saw some half dozen Dyaks preparing to quit her upon the opposite side. They were the last of the boarding party – the girl was nowhere in sight. Without waiting for his men the young giant sprang across the deck. His one thought was to find Virginia Maxon.

At the sound of his approach the Dyaks turned, and at the sight of a pajama clad white man armed only with a long whip they emitted savage cries of anticipation, counting the handsome trophy upon the white man's shoulders as already theirs. Number Thirteen would have paid no attention whatever to them had they not molested him, for the wished only to reach the girl's side as quickly as possible; but in another moment he found himself confronted by a half dozen dancing wild men, brandishing wicked looking parangs, and crying tauntingly.

Up went the great bull whip, and without abating his speed a particle the man leaped into the midst of the wicked blades that menaced him. Right and left with the quickness of thought the heavy lash fell upon heads, shoulders and sword arms. There was no chance to wield a blade in the face of that terrific onslaught, for the whip fell, not with the ordinary force of a man-held lash, but with all the stupendous power of those giant shoulders and arms behind it.

A single blow felled the foremost head hunter, breaking his shoulder and biting into the flesh and bone as a heavy sword bites. Again and again the merciless leather fell, while in the boats below Muda Saffir and his men shouted loud cries of encouragement to their companions on the ship, and a wide-eyed girl in the stern of Muda Saffir's own prahu looked on in terror, hope and admiration at the man of her own race whom she felt was battling against all these odds for her alone.

Virginia Maxon recognized her champion instantly as he who had fought for and saved her once before, from the hideous creature of her father's experiments. With hands tight pressed against her bosom the girl leaned forward, tense with excitement, watching every move of the lithe, giant figure, as, silhouetted against the brazen tropic sky, it towered above the dancing, shrieking head hunters who writhed beneath the awful lash.

Muda Saffir saw that the battle was going against his men, and it filled him with anger. Turning to one of his headmen he ordered two more boatloads of warriors to the Ithaca's deck. As they were rushing to obey their leader's command there was a respite in the fighting on the ship, for the three who had not fallen beneath the bull whip had leaped overboard to escape the fate which had overtaken their comrades.

As the reinforcements started to scale the vessel's side Number Thirteen's searching eyes found the girl in Muda Saffir's prahu, where it lay a little off from the Ithaca and as the first of the enemy clambered over the rail she saw a smile of encouragement light the clear cut features of the man above her. Virginia Maxon sent back an answering smile – a smile that filled the young giant's heart with pride and happiness – such a smile as brave men have been content to fight and die for since woman first learned the art of smiling.

Number Thirteen could have beaten back many of the reinforcing party before they reached the deck, but he did not care to do so. In the spontaneous ethics of the man there seemed no place for an unfair advantage over an enemy, and added to this was his newly acquired love of battle, so he was content to wait until his foes stood on an even footing with him before he engaged them. But they never came within reach of his ready lash. Instead, as they came above the ship's side they paused, wide-eyed and terror stricken, and with cries of fear and consternation dropped precipitately back into the sea, shouting warnings to those who were about to scale the hull.

Muda Saffir arose in his prahu cursing and reviling the frightened Dyaks. He did not know the cause of their alarm, but presently he saw it behind the giant upon the Ithaca's deck – eleven horrible monstrosities lumbering forward, snarling and growling, to their leader's side.

At the sight his own dark countenance went ashen, and with trembling lips he ordered his oarsmen to pull for the open sea. The girl, too, saw the frightful creatures that surrounded the man upon the deck. She thought that they were about to attack him, and gave a little cry of warning, but in another instant she realized that they were his companions, for with him they rushed to the side of the ship to stand for a moment looking down upon the struggling Dyaks in the water below.

Two prahus lay directly beneath them, and into these the head hunters were scrambling. The balance of the flotilla was now making rapid headway under oars and sail toward the mouth of the harbor, and as Number Thirteen saw that the girl was being borne away from him, he shouted a command to his misshapen crew, and without waiting to see if they would follow him leaped into the nearer of the two boats beneath.

It was already half filled with Dyaks, some of whom were hastily manning the oars. Others of the head hunters were scrambling over the gunwale. In an instant pandemonium reigned in the little vessel. Savage warriors sprang toward the tall figure towering above them. Parangs flashed. The bull whip hissed and cracked, and then into the midst of it all came a horrid avalanche of fearful and grotesque monsters – the young giant's crew had followed at his command.

The battle in the prahu was short and fierce. For an instant the Dyaks attempted to hold their own, but in the face of the snarling, rending horde that engulfed them terror got the better of them all, so that those who were not overcome dived overboard and swam rapidly toward shore.

The other prahu had not waited to assist its companion, but before it was entirely filled had gotten under way and was now rapidly overhauling the balance of the fleet.

Von Horn had been an excited witness to all that had occurred upon the tranquil bosom of the little harbor. He had been filled with astonishment at sight of the inhabitants of the court of mystery fighting under the leadership of Number Thirteen, and now he watched interestedly the outcome of the adventure.

The sight of the girl being borne away in the prahu of the Malay rajah to a fate worse than death, had roused in him both keen regret and savage rage, but it was the life of ease that he was losing that concerned him most. He had felt so sure of winning Professor Maxon's fortune through either a forced or voluntary marriage with the girl that his feelings now were as of one whose rightful heritage has been foully wrested from him. The thought of the girl's danger and suffering were of but secondary consideration to him, for the man was incapable of either deep love or true chivalry.

Quite the contrary were the emotions which urged on the soulless creature who now found himself in undisputed possession of a Dyak war prahu. His only thought was of the girl being rapidly borne away across the glimmering waters of the strait. He knew not to what dangers she was exposed, or what fate threatened her. All he knew was that she had been taken by force against her will. He had seen the look of terror in her eyes, and the dawning hope die out as the boat that carried her had turned rapidly away from the Ithaca. His one thought now was to rescue her from her abductors and return her to her father. Of his own reward or profit he entertained no single thought – it was enough if he could fight for her. That would be reward sufficient.

Neither Number Thirteen nor any of his crew had ever before seen a boat, and outside the leader there was scarcely enough brains in the entire party to render it at all likely that they could ever navigate it, but the young man saw that the other prahus were being propelled by the long sticks which protruded from their sides, and he also saw the sails bellying with wind, though he had but a vague conception of their purpose.

For a moment he stood watching the actions of the men in the nearest boat, and then he set himself to the task of placing his own men at the oars and instructing them in the manner of wielding the unfamiliar implements. For an hour he worked with the brainless things that constituted his party. They could not seem to learn what was required of them. The paddles were continually fouling one another, or being merely dipped into the water and withdrawn without the faintest semblance of a stroke made.

The tiresome maneuvering had carried them about in circles back and forth across the harbor, but by it Number Thirteen had himself learned something of the proper method of propelling and steering his craft. At last, more through accident than intent, they came opposite the mouth of the basin, and then chance did for them what days of arduous endeavor upon their part might have failed to accomplish.

As they hung wavering in the opening, the broad strait before them, and their quarry fast diminishing to small specks upon the distant horizon, a vagrant land breeze suddenly bellyed the flapping sail. The prahu swung quickly about with nose pointed toward the sea, the sail filled, and the long, narrow craft shout out of the harbor and sped on over the dancing waters in the wake of her sisters.

On shore behind them the infuriated Dyaks who had escaped to the beach danced and shrieked; von Horn, from his hiding place, looked on in surprised wonder, and Bududreen's lascar cursed the fate that had left a party of forty head hunters upon the same small island with him.

Smaller and smaller grew the retreating prahu as, straight as an arrow, she sped toward the dim outline of verdure clad Borneo.

IX

INTO SAVAGE BORNEO

Von Horn cursed the chance that had snatched the girl from
him, but he tried to content himself with the thought that the
treasure probably still rested in the cabin of the Ithaca, where
Bududreen was to have deposited it. He wished that the Dyaks
would take themselves off so that he could board the vessel
and carry the chest ashore to bury it against the time that fate
should provide a means for transporting it to Singapore.

In the water below him floated the Ithaca's masts, their grisly
burdens still lashed to their wave swept sides. Bududreen lay
there, his contorted features set in a horrible grimace of death
which grinned up at the man he would have cheated, as though
conscious of the fact that the white man would have betrayed
him had the opportunity come, the while he enjoyed in anticipation the other's disappointment in the loss of both the girl
and the treasure.

The tide was rising now, and presently the Ithaca began to
float. No sooner was it apparent that she was free than the
Dyaks sprang into the water and swam to her side. Like mon-
keys they scrambled aboard, swarming below deck in search,
thought von Horn, of pillage. He prayed that they would not
discover the chest.

Presently a half dozen of them leaped overboard and swam
to the mass of tangled spars and rigging which littered the
beach. Selecting what they wished they returned to the vessel,
and a few minutes later von Horn was chagrined to see them
stepping a jury mast – he thought the treasure lay in the
Ithaca's cabin.

Before dark the vessel moved slowly out of the harbor, setting a course across the strait in the direction that the war
prahus had taken. When it was apparent that there was no
danger that the head hunters would return, the lascar came from
his hiding place, and dancing up and down upon the shore
screamed warlike challenges and taunts at the retreating enemy.

Von Horn also came forth, much to the sailor's surprise, and in silence the two stood watching the disappearing ship. At length they turned and made their way up the stream toward camp – there was no longer aught to fear there. Von Horn wondered if the creatures he had loosed upon Professor Maxon had done their work before they left, or if they had all turned to mush as had Number Thirteen.

Once at the encampment his questions were answered, for he saw a light in the bungalow, and as he mounted the steps there were Sing and Professor Maxon just coming from the living room.

'Von Horn!' exclaimed the professor. 'You, then, are not dead; but where is Virginia? Tell me that she is safe.'

'She has been carried away,' was the startling answer. 'Your creatures, under the thing you wished to marry her to, have taken her to Borneo with a band of Malay and Dyak pirates. I was alone and could do nothing to prevent them.'

'God!' moaned the old man. 'Why did I not kill the thing when it stood within my power to do so. Only last night he was here beside me, and now it is too late.'

'I warned you,' said von Horn, coldly.

'I was mad,' retorted the professor. 'Could you not see that I was mad? Oh, why did you not stop me? You were sane enough. You at least might have forced me to abandon the insane obsession which has overpowered my reason for all these terrible months. I am sane now, but it is too late – too late.'

'Both you and your daughter could only have interpreted any such action on my part as instigated by self-interest, for you both knew that I wanted to make her my wife,' replied the other. 'My hands were tied. I am sorry now that I did not act, but you can readily see the position in which I was placed.'

'Can nothing be done to get her back?' cried the father. 'There must be some way to save her. Do it von Horn, and not only is my daughter yours but my wealth as well – every thing that I possess shall be yours if you will but save her from those frightful creatures.'

'The Ithaca is gone, too,' replied the doctor. 'There is only a small boat that I hid in the jungle for some such emergency. It will carry us to Borneo, but what can we four do against five hundred pirates and the dozen monsters you have brought into the world? No, Professor Maxon, I fear there is little hope, though I am willing to give my life in an attempt to save

Virginia. You will not forget your promise should we succeed?'

'No, doctor,' replied the old man. 'I swear that you shall have Virginia as your wife, and all my property shall be made over to you if she is rescued.'

Sing Lee had been a silent listener to this strange conversation. An odd look came into his slant eyes as he heard von Horn exact a confirmation from the professor, but what passed in his shrewd mind only he could say.

It was too late to attempt to make a start that day for Borneo, as darkness had already fallen. Professor Maxon and von Horn walked over to the workshop and the inner campong to ascertain what damage had been done there.

On their return Sing was setting the table on the verandah for the evening meal. The two men were talking, and without making his presence noticeable the Chinaman hovered about ever within ear shot.

'I cannot make it out, von Horn,' Professor Maxon was saying. 'Not a board broken, and the doors both apparently opened intentionally by someone familiar with locks and bolts. Who could have done it?'

'You forget Number Thirteen,' suggested the doctor.

'But the chest!' expostulated the other. 'What in the world would he want of that enormous and heavy chest?'

'He might have thought that it contained treasure,' hazarded von Horn, in an innocent tone of voice.

'Bosh, my dear man,' replied Professor Maxon. 'He knew nothing of treasures, or money, or the need or value of either. I tell you the workshop was opened, and the inner campong as well by some one who knew the value of money and wanted that chest, but why they should have released the creatures from the inner enclosure is beyond me.'

'And I tell you Professor Maxon that it could have been none other than Number Thirteen,' insisted von Horn. Did I not myself see him leading his eleven monsters as easily as a captain commands his company. The fellow is brighter than we have imagined. He has learned much from us both, he has reasoned, and he has shrewdly guessed many things that he could not have known through experience.'

'But his object?' asked the professor.

'That is simple,' returned von Horn. 'You have held out hopes to him that soon he should come to live under your roof

85

with Virginia. The creature has been madly infatuated with her ever since the day he took her from Number One, and you have encouraged his infatuation until yesterday. Then you regained your sanity and put him in his rightful place. What is the result? Denied the easy prey he expected he immediately decided to take it by force, and with that end in view, and taking advantage of the series of remarkable circumstances which played into his hands, he liberated his fellows, and with them hastened to the beach in search of Virginia and in hopes of being able to fly with her upon the Ithaca. There he met the Malay pirates, and together they formed an alliance under terms of which Number Thirteen is to have the girl, and the pirates the chest in return for transporting him and his crew to Borneo. Why it is all perfectly simple and logical, Professor Maxon; do you not see it now?'

'You may be right, doctor,' answered the old man. 'But it is idle to conjecture. Tomorrow we can be up and doing, so let us get what sleep we can tonight. We shall need all our energies if we are to save my poor, dear girl, from the clutches of that horrid, soulless thing.'

At the very moment that he spoke the object of his contumely was entering the dark mouth of a broad river that flowed from out of the heart of savage Borneo. In the prahu with him his eleven hideous companions now bent to their paddles with slightly increased efficiency. Before them the leader saw a fire blazing upon a tiny island in the center of the stream. Toward this they turned their silent way. Grimly the war prahu with its frightful freight nosed closer to the bank.

At last Number Thirteen made out the figures of men about the fire, and as they came still closer he was sure that they were members of the very party he had been pursuing across the broad waters for hours. The prahus were drawn up upon the bank and the warriors were preparing to eat.

Just as the young giant's prahu came within the circle of firelight a swarthy Malay approached the fire, dragging a white girl roughly by the arm. No more was needed to convince Number Thirteen of the identity of the party. With a low command to his fellows he urged them to redoubled speed. At the same instant a Dyak warrior caught sight of the approaching boat as it sped into the full glare of the light.

At sight of the occupants the head hunters scattered for their own prahus. The frightful aspect of the enemy turned their savage hearts to water, leaving no fight in their ordinarily warlike souls.

So quickly they moved that as the pursuing prahu touched the bank all the nearer boats had been launched, and the remaining pirates were scurrying across the little island for those which lay upon the opposite side. Among these was the Malay who guarded the girl, but he had not been quick enough to prevent Virginia Maxon recognizing the stalwart figure standing in the bow of the oncoming craft.

As he dragged her away toward the prahu of Muda Saffir she cried out to the strange white man who seemed her self-appointed protector.

'Help! Help!' she called. 'This way! Across the island!' And then the brown hand of her jailer closed over her mouth. Like a tigress she fought to free herself, or to detain her captor until the rescue party should catch up with them, but the scoundrel was muscled like a bull, and when the girl held back he lifted her across his shoulder and broke into a run.

Rajah Muda Saffir had no stomach for a fight himself, but he was loathe to lose his prize he had but just won, and seeing that his men were panic-stricken he saw no alternative but to rally them for a brief stand that would give the little moment required to slip away in his own prahu with the girl.

Calling aloud for those around him to come to his support he halted fifty yards from his boat just as Number Thirteen with his fierce, brainless horde swept up from the opposite side of the island in the wake of him who bore Virginia Maxon. The old rajah succeeded in gathering some fifty warriors about him from the crews of the two boats which lay near his. His own men he hastened to their posts in his prahu that they might be ready to pull swiftly away the moment that he and the captive were aboard.

The Dyak warriors presented an awe inspiring spectacle in the fitful light of the nearby camp fire. The ferocity of their fierce faces was accentuated by the upturned, bristling tiger-cat's teeth which protruded from every ear; while the long feathers of the Argus pheasant waving from their warcaps, the brilliant colors of their war-coats trimmed with the black and white feathers of the hornbill, and the strange devices upon their gaudy shields but added to the savagery of their appearance as they danced and howled, menacing and intimidating, in the path of the charging foe.

A single backward glance was all that Virginia Maxon found it possible to throw in the direction of the rescue party, and in that she saw a sight that lived forever in her memory. At the head of his hideous, misshapen pack sprang the stalwart young giant straight into the heart of the flashing parangs of the howling savages. To right and left fell the mighty bull whip cutting down men with all the force and dispatch of a steel saber. The Dyaks, encouraged by the presence of Muda Saffir in their rear, held their ground; and the infuriated, brainless things that followed the wielder of the bull whip threw themselves upon the head hunters with beating hands and rending fangs.

Number Ten wrested a parang from an adversary, and acting upon his example the other creatures were not long in arming themselves in a similar manner. Cutting and jabbing they hewed their way through the solid ranks of the enemy, until Muda Saffir, seeing that defeat was inevitable turned and fled toward his prahu.

Four of his creatures lay dead as the last of the Dyaks turned to escape from the mad white man who faced naked steel with only a rawhide whip. In panic the headhunters made a wild dash for the two remaining prahus, for Muda Saffir had succeeded in getting away from the island in safety.

Number Thirteen reached the water's edge but a moment after the prow of the rajah's craft had cleared the shore and was swinging up stream under the vigorous strokes of its fifty oarsmen. For an instant he stood poised upon the bank as though to spring after the retreating prahu, but the knowledge that he could not swim held him back – it was useless to throw away his life when the need of it was so great if Virginia Maxon was to be saved.

Turning to the other prahus he saw that one was already launched, but that the crew of the other was engaged in a desperate battle with the seven remaining members of his crew for possession of the boat. Leaping among the combatants he urged his fellows aboard the prahu which was already half-filled with Dyaks. Then he shoved the boat out into the river, jumping aboard himself as its prow cleared the gravelly beach.

For several minutes that long, hollowed log was a veritable floating hell of savage, screaming men locked in deadly battle. The sharp parangs of the head hunters were no match for the superhuman muscles of the creatures that battered them about; now lifting one high above his fellows and using the body as a club to beat down those nearby; again snapping an arm or a leg as one might break a pipe stem; or hurling a living antagonist headlong above the heads of his fellows to the dark waters of the river. And above them all in the thickest of the fight, towering even above his own giants, rose the mighty figure of the terrible white man, whose very presence wrought havoc with the valor of the brown warriors.

Two more of Number Thirteen's creatures had been cut down in the prahu, but the loss among the Dyaks had been infinitely greater, and to it was now added the desertions of the terror stricken savages who seemed to fear the frightful countenances of their adversaries even as much as they did their prowess.

There remained but a handful of brown warriors in one end of the boat when the advantage of utilizing their knowledge of the river and of navigation occurred to Number Thirteen. Calling to his men he commanded them to cease killing, making prisoners of those who remained instead. So accustomed had his pack now become to receiving and acting upon his orders that they changed their tactics immediately, and one by one the remaining Dyaks were overpowered, disarmed and held.

With difficulty Number Thirteen communicated with them, for among them there was but a single warrior who had ever had intercourse with an Englishman, but at last by means of signs and the few words that were common to them both he made the native understand that he would spare the lives of himself and his companions if they would help him in pursuit of Muda Saffir and the girl.

The Dyaks felt but little loyalty for the rascally Malay they served, since in common with all their kind they and theirs had suffered for generations at the hands of the cruel, crafty and unscrupulous race that had usurped the administration of their land. So it was not difficult to secure from them the promise of assistance in return for their lives.

Number Thirteen noticed that when they addressed him it was always as Bulan, and upon questioning them he discovered that they had given him this title of honor partly in view of his wonderful fighting ability and partly because the sight of his white face emerging from out of the darkness of the river into the firelight of their blazing camp fire had carried to their impressionable minds a suggestion of the tropic moon which they admired and reverenced. Both the name and the idea appealed to Number Thirteen and from that time he adopted Bulan as his rightful cognomen.

The loss of time resulting from the fight in the prahu and the ensuing peace parley permitted Muda Saffir to put considerable distance between himself and his pursuers. The Malay's boat was now alone, for of the eight prahus that remained of the original fleet it was the only one which had taken this branch of the river, the others having scurried into a smaller southerly arm after the fight upon the island, that they might the more easily escape their hideous foemen.

Only Barunda, the headman, knew which channel Rajah Muda Saffir intended following, and Muda wondered why it was that the two boats that were to have borne Barunda's men did not catch up with his. While he had left Barunda and his warriors engaged in battle with the strangers he did not for an instant imagine that they would suffer any severe loss, and that one of their boats should be captured was beyond belief. But this was precisely what had happened, and the second boat, seeing the direction taken by the enemy, had turned down stream the more surely to escape them.

So it was that while Rajah Muda Saffir moved leisurely up the river toward his distant stronghold waiting for the other boats of his fleet to overtake him, Barunda, the headman, guided the white enemy swiftly after him. Barunda had discovered that it was the girl alone this white man wanted. Evidently he either knew nothing of the treasure chest lying in the bottom of Muda Saffir's boat, or, knowing, was indifferent. In either event Barunda thought that he saw a chance to possess himself of the rich contents of the heavy box, and so served his new master with much greater enthusiasm than he had the old.

Beneath the paddles of the natives and the five remaining members of his pack Bulan sped up the dark river after the single prahu with its priceless freight. Already six of the creatures of Professor Maxon's experiments had given up their lives in the service of his daughter, and the remaining six were pushing forward through the inky blackness of the jungle night into the untracked heart of savage Borneo to rescue her from her abductors though they sacrificed their own lives in the endeavor.

Far ahead of them in the bottom of the great prahu crouched the girl they sought. Her thoughts were of the man she felt intuitively to possess the strength, endurance and ability to overcome every obstacle and reach her at last. Would he come in time? Ah, that was the question. The mystery of the stranger appealed to her. A thousand times she had attempted to solve the question of his first appearance on the island, at the very moment that his mighty muscles were needed to rescue her from the horrible creature of her father's creation. Then there was his unaccountable disappearance for weeks; there was von Horn's strange reticence and seeming ignorance as to the circumstances which brought the young man to the island, or his equally unaccountable disappearance after having rescued her from Number One. And now, when she suddenly found herself in need of protection, here was the same young man turning up in a most miraculous fashion, and at the head of the terrible creatures of the inner campong.

The riddle was too deep for her – she could not solve it; and then her thoughts were interrupted by the thin, brown hand of Rajah Muda Saffir as it encircled her waist and drew her toward him. Upon the evil lips were hot words of passion. The girl wrenched herself from the man's embrace, and, with a little scream of terror, sprang to her feet, and as Muda Saffir arose to grasp her again she struck him full in the face with one small, clenched fist.

Directly behind the Malay lay the heavy chest of Professor Maxon. As the man stepped backward to recover his equilibrium both feet struck the object. For an instant he tottered with wildly waving arms in an endeavor to regain his lost balance, then, with a curse upon his lips, he lunged across the box and over the side of the prahu into the dark waters of the river.

X

DESPERATE CHANCE

The great chest in the bottom of Rajah Muda Saffir's prahu had awakened in other hearts as well as his, blind greed and avarice; so that as it had been the indirect cause of his disaster it now proved the incentive to another to turn the mishap to his own profit, and to the final undoing of the Malay.

The panglima Ninaka of the Signana Dyaks who manned Muda Saffir's war prahu saw his chief disappear beneath the swift waters of the river, but the word of command that would have sent the boat hurriedly back to pick up the swimmer was not given. Instead a lusty cry for greater speed ahead urged the sinuous muscles gliding beneath the sleek brown hides; and when Muda Saffir rose to the surface with a cry for help upon his lips Nanaka shouted back to him in derision, consigning his carcass to the belly of the nearest crocodile.

In futile rage Muda Saffir called down the most terrible curses of Allah and his Prophet upon the head of Ninaka and his progeny to the fifth generation, and upon the shades of his forefathers, and upon the grim skulls which hung from the rafters of his long-house. Then he turned and swam rapidly toward the shore.

Ninaka, now in possession of both the chest and the girl, was rich indeed, but with Muda Saffir dead he scarce knew to whom he could dispose of the white girl for a price that would make it worth while to be burdened with the danger and responsibility of retaining her. He had had some experience of white men in the past and knew that dire were the punishments meted to those who wronged the white man's woman. All through the remainder of the long night Ninaka pondered the question deeply. At last he turned to Virginia.

'Why does the big white man who leads the orang-outangs follow us?' he asked. 'Is it the chest he desires, or you?'

'It is certainly not the chest,' replied the girl. 'He wishes to take me back to my father, that is all. If you will return me to him you may keep the chest, if that is what you wish.'

Ninaka looked at her quizzically for a moment. Evidently then she was of some value. Possibly should he retain her he could wring a handsome ransom from the white man. He would wait and see, it were always an easy matter to rid himself of her should circumstances require. The river was there, deep, dark and silent, and he could place the responsibility for her loss upon Muda Saffir.

Shortly after day break Ninaka beached his prahu before the long-house of a peaceful river tribe. The chest he hid in the underbrush close by his boat, and with the girl ascended the notched log that led to the varandah of the structure, which, stretching away for three hundred yards upon its tall piles, resembled a huge centipede.

The dwellers in the long-house extended every courtesy to Ninaka and his crew. At the former's request Virginia was hidden away in a dark sleeping closet in one of the windowless living rooms which opened along the verandah for the full length of the house. Here a native girl brought her food and water, sitting, while she ate, in rapt contemplation of the white skin and golden hair of the strange female.

At about the time that Ninaka pulled his prahu upon the beach before the long-house Muda Saffir from the safety of the concealing underbrush upon the shore saw a familiar war prahu forging rapidly up the stream. As it approached him he was about to call aloud to those who manned it, for in the bow he saw a number of his own men; but a second glance as the boat came opposite him caused him to alter his intention and drop further into the engulfing verdure, for behind his men squatted five of the terrible monsters that had wrought such havoc with his expedition, and in the stern he saw his own Barunda in friendly converse with the mad white man who had led them.

As the boat disappeared about a bend in the river Rajah Muda Saffir arose, shaking his fist in the direction it had vanished and, cursing anew and volubly, damned each separate hair in the heads of the faithless Barunda and the traitorous Ninaka. Then he resumed his watch for the friendly prahu, or smaller sampan which he knew time would eventually bring from up or down the river to his rescue, for who of the surrounding natives would dare refuse succor to the powerful Rajah of Sakkan!

At the long-house which harbored Ninaka and his crew, Barunda and Bulan stopped with theirs to obtain food and rest. The quick eye of the Dyak chieftain recognized the prahu of Rajah Muda Saffir where it lay upon the beach, but he said nothing to his white companion of what it augured – it might be well to discover how the land lay before he committed himself too deeply to either faction.

At the top of the notched log he was met by Ninaka, who, with horror-wide eyes, looked down upon the fearsom monstrosities that lumbered awkwardly up the rude ladder in the wake of the agile Dyaks and the young white giant.

'What does it mean?' whispered the panglima to Barunda.

'These are now my friends,' replied Barunda. 'Where is Muda Saffir?'

Ninaka jerked his thumb toward the river. 'Some crocodile has feasted well,' he said significantly. Barunda smiled.

'And the girl?' he continued. 'And the treasure?'

Ninaka's eyes narrowed. 'They are safe,' he answered.

'The white man wants the girl,' remarked Barunda. 'He does not suspect that you are one of Muda Saffir's people. If he guessed that you knew the whereabouts of the girl he would torture the truth from you and then kill you. He does not care for the treasure. There is enough in that great chest for two, Ninaka. Let us be friends. Together we can divide it; otherwise neither of us will get any of it. What do you say, Ninaka?'

The panglima scowled. He did not relish the idea of sharing his prize, but he was shrewd enough to realize that Barunda possessed the power to rob him of it all, so at last he acquiesced, though with poor grace.

Bulan had stood near during the conversation, unable, of course, to understand a single word of the native tongue.

'What does the man say?' he asked Barunda. 'Has he seen anything of the prahu bearing the girl?'

'Yes,' replied the Dyak. 'He says that two hours ago such a war prahu passed on its way up river – he saw the white girl plainly. Also he knows whither they are bound, and how, by crossing through the jungle on foot, you may intercept them at their next stop.'

Bulan, suspecting no treachery, was all anxiety to be off at once. Barunda suggested that in case of some possible emergency causing the quarry to return down the river it would be well to have a force remain at the long-house to intercept them. He volunteered to undertake the command of this party. Ninaka, he said, would furnish guides to escort Bulan and his men through the jungle to the point at which they might expect to find Muda Saffir.

And so, with the girl he sought lying within fifty feet of him, Bulan started off through the jungle with two of Ninaka's Dyaks as guides – guides who had been well instructed by their panglima as to their duties. Twisting and turning through the dense maze of underbrush and close-growing, lofty trees the little party of eight plunged farther and farther into the bewildering labyrinth.

For hours the tiresome march was continued, until at last the guides halted, apparently to consult each other as to the proper direction. By signs they made known to Bulan that they did not agree upon the right course to pursue from there on, and that they had decided that it would be best for each to advance a little way in the direction he thought the right one while Bulan and his five creatures remained where they were.

'We will go but a little way,' said the spokesman, 'and then we shall return and lead you in the proper direction.'

Bulan saw no harm in this, and without a shade of suspicion sat down upon a fallen tree and watched his two guides disappear into the jungle in opposite directions. Once out of sight of the white man the two turned back and met a short distance in the rear of the party they had deserted – in another moment they were headed for the long-house from which they had started.

It was fully an hour thereafter that doubts began to enter Bulan's head, and as the day dragged on he came to realize that he and his weird pack were alone and lost in the heart of a strange and tangled web of tropical jungle.

No sooner had Bulan and his party disappeared in the jungle than Barunda and Ninaka made haste to embark with the chest and the girl and push rapidly on up the river toward the wild and inaccessible regions of the interior. Virginia Maxon's strong hope of succor had been gradually waning as no sign of the rescue party appeared as the day wore on. Somewhere behind her upon the broad river she was sure a long, narrow native prahu was being urged forward in pursuit, and that in command of it was the young giant who was now never for a moment absent from her thoughts.

For hours she strained her eyes over the stern of the craft that was bearing her deeper and deeper into the wilder heart of fierce Borneo. On either shore they occasionally passed a native long-house, and the girl could not help but wonder at the quiet and peace which reigned over these little settlements. It was as though they were passing along a beaten highway in the center of a civilized community; and yet she knew that the men who lolled upon the verandahs, puffing indolently upon their cigarettes or chewing betel nut, were all head hunters, and that along the verandah rafters above them hung the grisly trophies of their prowess.

Yet as she glanced from them to her new captors she could not but feel that she would prefer captivity in one of the settlements they were passing – there at least she might find an opportunity to communicate with her father, or be discovered by the rescue party as it came up the river. The idea grew upon her as the day advanced until she spent the time in watching furtively for some means of escape should they but touch the shore momentarily; and though they halted twice her captors were too watchful to permit her the slightest opportunity for putting her plan into action.

Barunda and Ninaka urged their men on, with brief rests, all day, nor did they halt even after night had closed down upon the river. On, on the swift prahu sped up the winding channel which had now dwindled to a narrow stream, at intervals rushing strongly between rocky walls with a current that tested the strength of the strong, brown paddlers.

Long-houses had become more and more infrequent until for some time now no sign of human habitation had been visible. The jungle undergrowth was scantier and the spaces between the boles of the forest trees more open. Virginia Maxon was almost frantic with despair as the utter helplessness of her position grew upon her. Each stroke of those slender paddles was driving her farther and farther from friends, or the possibility of rescue. Night had fallen, dark and impenetrable, and with it had come the haunting fears that creep in when the sun has deserted his guardian post.

Barunda and Ninaka were whispering together in low gutturals, and to the girl's distorted and fear excited imagination it seemed possible that she alone must be the subject of their plotting. The prahu was gliding through a stretch of comparatively quiet and placid water where the stream spread out into a little basin just above a narrow gorge through which they had just forced their way by dint of the most laborious exertions on the part of the crew.

Virginia watched the two men near her furtively. They were deeply engrossed in their conversation. Neither was looking in her direction. The backs of the paddlers were all toward her. Stealthily she rose to a stooping position at the boat's side. For a moment she paused, and then, almost noiselessly, dove overboard and disappeared beneath the black waters.

It was the slight rocking of the prahu that caused Barunda to look suddenly about to discover the reason for the disturbance. For a moment neither of the men apprehended the girl's absence. Ninaka was the first to do so, and it was he who called loudly to the paddlers to bring the boat to a stop. Then they dropped down the river with the current, and paddled about above the gorge for half an hour.

The moment that Virginia Maxon felt the waters close above her head she struck out beneath the surface for the shore upon the opposite side to that toward which she had dived into the river. She knew that if any had seen her leave the prahu they would naturally expect to intercept her on her way toward the nearest shore, and so she took this means of outwitting them, although it meant nearly double the distance to be covered.

After swimming a short distance beneath the surface the girl rose and looked about her. Up the river a few yards she caught the phosphorescent gleam of water upon the prahu's paddles as they brought her to a sudden stop in obedience to Ninaka's command. Then she saw the dark mass of the war-craft drifting down toward her.

Again she dove and with strong strokes headed for the shore. The next time that she rose she was terrified to see the prahu looming close behind her. The paddlers were propelling the boat slowly in her direction – it was almost upon her now – there was a shout from a man in the bow – she had been seen.

Like a flash she dove once more and, turning, struck out rapidly straight back beneath the oncoming boat. When she came to the surface again it was to find herself as far from shore as she had been when she first quitted the prahu, but the craft was now circling far below her, and she set out once again to retrace her way toward the inky mass of shore line which loomed apparently near and yet, as she knew, was some considerable distance from her.

As she swam, her mind, filled with the terrors of the night, conjured recollection of the stories she had heard of the fierce crocodiles which infest certain of the rivers of Borneo. Again and again she could have sworn that she felt some huge, slimy body sweep beneath her in the mysterious waters of this un-known river.

Behind her she saw the prahu turn back up stream, but now her mind was suddenly engaged with a new danger, for the girl realized that the strong current was bearing her down stream more rapidly than she had imagined. Already she could hear the increasing roar of the river as it rushed, wild and tumultuous, through the entrance to the narrow gorge below her. How far it was to the shore she could not guess, or how far to the certain death of the swirling waters toward which she was being drawn by an irresistible force; but of one thing she was certain, her strength was rapidly waning, and she must reach the bank quickly.

With redoubled energy she struck out in one last mighty effort to reach the shore. The tug of the current was strong upon her, like a giant hand reaching up out of the cruel river to bear her back to death. She felt her strength ebbing quickly – her strokes now were feeble and futile. With a prayer to her Maker she threw her hands above her head in the last effort of the drowning swimmer to clutch at even thin air for sup-port – the current caught and swirled her downward toward the gorge, and at the same instant her fingers touched and closed upon something which swung low above the water.

With the last flickering spark of vitality that remained in her poor, exhausted body Virginia Maxon clung to the frail support that a kind Providence had thrust into her hands. How long she hung there she never knew, but finally a little strength returned to her, and presently she realized that it was a pendant creeper hanging low from a jungle tree upon the bank that had saved her from the river's rapacious maw.

Inch by inch she worked herself upward toward the bank, and at last, weak and panting, sunk exhausted to the cool carpet of grass that grew to the water's edge. Almost immediately tired Nature plunged her into a deep sleep. It was daylight when she awoke, dreaming that the tall young giant had rescued her from a band of demons and was lifting her in his arms to carry her back to her father.

Through half open lids she saw the sunlight filtering through the leafy canopy above her – she wondered at the realism of her dream; full consciousness returned and with it the conviction that she was in truth being held close by strong arms against a bosom that throbbed to the beating of a real heart.

With a sudden start she opened her eyes wide to look up into the hideous face of a giant orang-outang.

XI

'I AM COMING'

The morning following the capture of Virginia Maxon by Muda Saffir, Professor Maxon, von Horn, Sing Lee and the sole surviving lascar from the crew of the Ithaca set out across the strait toward the mainland of Borneo in the small boat which the doctor had secreted in the jungle near the harbor. The party was well equipped with firearms and ammunition, and the bottom of the boat was packed full with provisions and cooking utensils. Von Horn had been careful to see that the boat was furnished with a mast and sail, and now, under a good breeze the party was making excellent time toward the mysterious land of their destination.

They had scarcely cleared the harbor when they sighted a ship far out across the strait. Its erratic movements riveted their attention upon it, and later, as they drew nearer, they perceived that the strange craft was a good sized schooner with but a single short mast and tiny sail. For a minute or two her sail would belly with the wind and the vessel make headway, then she would come suddenly about, only to repeat the same tactics a moment later. She sailed first this way and then that, losing one minute what she had gained the minute before.

Von Horn was the first to recognize her.

'It is the Ithaca,' he said, 'and her Dyak crew are having a devil of a time managing her – she acts as though she were rudderless.'

Von Horn ran the small boat within hailing distance of the dismasted hulk whose side was now lined with waving, gesticulating natives. They were peaceful fishermen, they explained, whose prahus had been wrecked in the recent typhoon. They had barely escaped with their lives by clambering aboard this wreck which Allah had been so merciful as to place directly in their road. Would the Tuan Besar be so good as to tell them how to make the big prahu steer?

Von Horn promised to help them on condition that they would guide him and his party to the stronghold of Rajah Muda

Saffir in the heart of Borneo. The Dyaks willingly agreed, and von Horn worked his small boat in close under the Ithaca's stern. Here he found that the rudder had been all but unshipped, probably as the vessel was lifted over the reef during the storm; but a single pintle remaining in its gudgeon. A half hour's work was sufficient to repair the damage, and then the two boats continued their journey toward the mouth of the river up which those they sought had passed the night before.

Inside the river's mouth an anchorage was found for the Ithaca near the very island upon which the fierce battle between Number Thirteen and Muda Saffir's forces had occurred. From the deck of the larger vessel the deserted prahu which had borne Bulan across the strait was visible, as were the bodies of the slain Dyaks and the misshapen creatures of the white giant's forces.

In excited tones the head hunters called von Horn's attention to these evidences of conflict, and the doctor drew his boat up to the island and leaped ashore, followed by Professor Maxon and Sing. Here they found the dead bodies of the four monsters who had fallen in an attempt to rescue their creator's daughter, though little did any there imagine the real truth.

About the corpses of the four were the bodies of a dozen Dyak warriors attesting the ferocity of the encounter and the savage prowess of the unarmed creatures who had sold their poor lives so dearly.

'Evidently they fell out about the possession of the captive,' suggested von Horn. 'Let us hope that she did not fall into the clutches of Number Thirteen – any fate would be better than that.'

'God give that that has not befallen her,' moaned Professor Maxon. 'The pirates might but hold her for ransom, but should that soulless fiend possess her my prayer is that she found the strength and the means to take her own life before he had an opportunity to have his way with her.'

'Amen,' agreed von Horn.

Sing Lee said nothing, but in his heart he hoped that Virginia Maxon was not in the power of Rajah Muda Saffir. The brief experience he had had with Number Thirteen during the fight in the bungalow had rather warmed his wrinkled old heart toward the friendless young giant, and he was a sufficiently good judge of human nature to be confident that the girl would be comparatively safe in his keeping.

It was quickly decided to abandon the small boat and embark the entire party in the deserted war prahu. A half hour later saw the strangely mixed expedition forging up the river, but not until von Horn had boarded the Ithaca and discovered to his dismay that the chest was not on board her.

Far above them on the right bank Muda Saffir still squatted in his hiding place, for no friendly prahu or sampan had passed his way since dawn. His keen eyes roving constantly up and down the long stretch of river that was visible from his position finally sighted a war prahu coming toward him from down stream. As it drew closer, he recognized it as one which had belonged to his own fleet before his unhappy encounter with the wild white man and his abhorrent pack, and a moment later his heart leaped as he saw the familiar faces of several of his men; but who were the strangers in the stern, and what was a Chinaman doing perched there upon the bow?

The prahu was nearly opposite him before he recognized Professor Maxon and von Horn as the white men of the little island. He wondered how much they knew of his part in the raid upon their encampment. Bududreen had told him much concerning the doctor, and as Muda Saffir recalled the fact that von Horn was anxious to possess himself of both the treasure and the girl he guessed that he would be safe in the man's hands so long as he could hold out promises of turning one or the other over to him; and so, as he was tired of squatting upon the uncomfortable bank and was very hungry, he arose and hailed the passing prahu.

His men recognized his voice immediately and as they knew nothing of the defection of any of their fellows, turned the boat's prow toward shore without waiting for the command from von Horn. The latter fearing treachery, sprang to his feet with raised rifle, but when one of the paddlers explained that it was the Rajah Muda Saffir who hailed them and that he was alone von Horn permitted them to draw nearer the shore, though he continued to stand ready to thwart any attempted treachery and warned both the professor and Sing to be on guard.

As the prahu's nose touched the bank Muda Saffir stepped aboard and with many protestations of gratitude explained that he had fallen overboard from his own prahu the night before and that evidently his followers thought him drowned, since none of his boats had returned to search for him. Scarcely had the Malay seated himself before von Horn began questioning him in the rajah's native tongue, not a word of which was intelligible to Professor Maxon. Sing, however, was as familiar with it as was von Horn.

'Where are the girl and the treasure?' he asked.

'What girl, Tuan Besar,' inquired the wily Malay innocently. 'And what treasure? The white man speaks in riddles.'

'Come, come,' cried von Horn impatiently. 'Let us have no foolishness. You know perfectly well what I mean – it will go far better with you if we work together as friends. I want the girl – if she is unharmed – and I will divide the treasure with you if you will help me to obtain them; otherwise you shall have no part of either. What do you say? Shall we be friends or enemies?'

'The girl and the treasure were both stolen from me by a rascally panglima, Ninaka,' said Muda Saffir, seeing that it would be as well to simulate friendship for the white man for the time being at least – there would always be an opportunity to use a kriss upon him in the remote fastness of the interior to which Muda Saffir would lead them.

'What became of the white man who led the strange monsters?' asked von Horn.

'He killed many of my men, and the last I saw of him he was pushing up the river after the girl and the treasure,' replied the Malay.

'If another should ask you,' continued von Horn with a meaning glance toward Professor Maxon, 'it will be well to say that the girl was stolen by this white giant and that you suffered defeat in an attempt to rescue her because of your friendship for us. Do you understand?'

Muda Saffir nodded. Here was a man after his own heart, which loved intrigue and duplicity. Evidently he would be a good ally in wreaking vengeance upon the white giant who had caused all his discomfiture – afterward there was always the kriss if the other should become inconvenient.

At the long-house at which Barunda and Ninaka had halted, Muda Saffir learned all that had transpired, his informants being the two Dyaks who had led Bulan and his pack into the jungle. He imparted the information to von Horn and both men were delighted that thus their most formidable enemy had been disposed of. It would be but a question of time before the inexperienced creatures perished in the dense forest – that they ever could retrace their steps to the river was most unlikely, and the chances were that one by one they would be dispatched by head hunters while they slept.

Again the party embarked, reinforced by the two Dyaks who were only too glad to renew their allegiance to Muda Saffir while he was backed by the guns of the white men. On and on they paddled up the river, gleaning from the dwellers in the various long-houses information of the passing of the two prahus with Barunda, Ninaka, and the white girl.

Professor Maxon was impatient to hear every detail that von Horn obtained from Muda Saffir and the various Dyaks that were interviewed at the first long-house and along the stretch of river they covered. The doctor told him that Number Thirteen still had Virginia and was fleeing up the river in a swift prahu. He enlarged upon the valor shown by Muda Saffir and his men in their noble attempt to rescue his daughter, and through it all Sing Lee sat with half closed eyes, apparently oblivious to all that passed before him. What were the workings of that intricate celestial brain none can say.

Far in the interior of the jungle Bulan and his five monsters stumbled on in an effort to find the river. Had they known it they were moving parallel with the stream, but a few miles from it. At times it wound in wide detours close to the path of the lost creatures, and again it circled far away from them.

As they travelled they subsisted upon the fruits with which they had become familiar upon the island of their creation. They suffered greatly for lack of water, but finally stumbled upon a small stream at which they filled their parched stomachs. Here it occurred to Bulan that it would be wise to follow the little river, since they could be no more completely lost than they now were no matter where it should lead them, and it would at least insure them plenty of fresh water.

As they proceeded down the bank of the stream it grew in size until presently it became a fair sized river, and Bulan had hopes that it might indeed prove the stream that they had ascended from the ocean and that soon he would meet with the prahus and possibly find Virginia Maxon herself. The strenuous march of the six through the jungle had torn their light cotton garments into shreds so that they were all practically naked, while their bodies were scratched and bleeding from countless wounds inflicted by sharp thorns and tangled brambles through which they had forced their way.

Bulan still carried his heavy bull whip while his five companions were armed with the parangs they had taken from the Dyaks they had overpowered upon the island at the mouth of the river. It was upon this strange and remarkable company that the sharp eyes of a score of river Dyaks peered through the foliage. The head hunters had been engaged in collecting camphor crystals when their quick ears caught the noisy passage of the six while yet at a considerable distance, and with ready parangs the savages crept stealthily toward the sound of the advancing party.

At first they were terror stricken at the hideous visages of five of the creatures they beheld, but when they saw how few their numbers, and how poorly armed they were, as well as the awkwardness with which they carried their parangs, denoting their unfamiliarity with the weapons, they took heart and prepared to ambush them.

What prizes those terrible heads would be when properly dried and decorated! The savages fairly trembled in anticipation of the commotion they would cause in the precincts of their long-house when they returned with six such magnificent trophies.

Their victims came blundering on through the dense jungle to where the twenty sleek brown warriors lay in wait for them. Bulan was in the lead, and close behind him in single file lumbered his awkward crew. Suddenly there was a chorus of savage cries close behind him and simultaneously he found himself in the midst of twenty cutting, slashing parangs.

Like lightning his bull whip flew into action, and to the astonished warriors it was as though a score of men were upon them in the person of this mighty white giant. Following the example of their leader the five creatures at his back leaped upon the nearest warriors, and though they wielded their parangs awkwardly the superhuman strength back of their cuts and thrusts sent the already blood stained blades through many a brown body.

The Dyaks would gladly have retreated after the first surprise of their initial attack, but Bulan urged his men on after them, and so they were forced to fight to preserve their lives at all. At last five of them managed to escape into the jungle, but fifteen remained quietly upon the earth where they had fallen – the victims of their own over confidence. Beside them lay two of Bulan's five, so that now the little party was reduced to four – and the problem that had faced Professor Maxon was so much closer to its own solution.

From the bodies of the dead Dyaks Bulan and his three companions, Number Three, Number Ten and Number Twelve, took enough loin cloths, caps, war-coats, shields and weapons to fit them out completely, after discarding the ragged remnants of their cotton pajamas, and now, even more terrible in appearance than before, the rapidly vanishing company of soulless monsters continued their aimless wandering down the river's brim.

The five Dyaks who had escaped carried the news of the terrible creatures that had fallen upon them in the jungle, and of the awful prowess of the giant white man who led them. They told of how, armed only with a huge whip, he had been a match and more than a match for the best warriors of the tribe, and the news that they started spread rapidly down the river from one long-house to another until it reached the broad stream into which the smaller river flowed, and then it travelled up and down to the headwaters above and the ocean far below in the remarkable manner that news travels in the wild places of the world.

So it was that as Bulan advanced he found the long-houses in his path deserted, and came to a larger river and turned up toward its head without meeting with resistance or even catching a glimpse of the brown-skinned people who watched him from their hiding places in the brush.

That night they slept in the long-house near the bank of the greater stream, while its rightful occupants made the best of it in the jungle behind. The next morning found the four again on the march ere the sun had scarcely lighted the dark places of the forest, for Bulan was now sure that he was on the right trail and that the new river that he had come to was indeed the same that he had traversed in the prahu with Barunda.

It must have been close to noon when the young giant's ears

caught the sound of the movement of some animal in the jungle a short distance to his right and away from the river. His experience with men had taught him to be wary, for it was evident that every man's hand was against him, so he determined to learn at once whether the noise he heard came from some human enemy lurking along his trail ready to spring upon him with naked parang at a moment that he was least prepared, or merely from some jungle brute.

Cautiously he threaded his way through the matted vegetation in the direction of the sound. Although a parang from the body of a vanquished Dyak hung at his side he grasped his bull whip ready in his right hand, preferring it to the less accustomed weapon of the head hunter. For a dozen yards he advanced without sighting the object of his search, but presently his efforts were rewarded by a glimpse of a reddish, hairy body, and a pair of close set, wicked eyes peering at him from behind a giant tree.

At the same instant a slight movement at one side attracted his attention to where another similar figure crouched in the underbrush, and then a third, fourth and fifth became evident about him. Bulan looked in wonderment upon the strange, man-like creatures who eyed him threateningly from every hand. They stood fully as high as the brown Dyak warriors, but their bodies were naked except for the growth of reddish hair which covered them, shading to black upon the face and hands.

The lips of the nearest were raised in an angry snarl that exposed wicked looking fighting fangs, but the beasts did not seem inclined to initiate hostilities, and as they were unarmed and evidently but engaged upon their own affairs Bulan decided to withdraw without arousing them further. As he turned to retrace his steps he found his three companions gazing in wide-eyed astonishment upon the strange new creatures which confronted them.

Number Ten was grinning broadly, while Number Three advanced cautiously toward one of the creatures, making a low guttural noise that could only be interpreted as peaceful and conciliatory — more like a feline purr it was than anything else.

'What are you doing?' cried Bulan. 'Leave them alone. They have not offered to harm us.'

'They are like us,' replied Number Three. 'They must be our own people. I am going with them.'

'And I,' said Number Ten.

'And I,' echoed Number Twelve. 'At last we have found our own, let us all go with them and live with them, far away from the men who would beat us with great whips, and cut us with their sharp swords.'

'They are not human beings,' exclaimed Bulan. 'We cannot live with them.'

'Neither are we human beings,' retorted Number Twelve. 'Has not von Horn told us so many times?'

'If I am not now a human being,' replied Bulan, 'I intend to be one, and so I shall act as a human being should act. I shall not go to live with savage beasts, nor shall you. Come with me as I tell you, or you shall again taste the bull whip.'

'We shall do as we please,' growled Number Ten, baring his fangs. 'You are not our master. We have followed you as long as we intend to. We are tired of forever walking, walking, walking through the bushes that tear our flesh and hurt us. Go and be a human being if you think you can, but do not longer interfere with us or we shall kill you,' and he looked first at Number Three and then at Number Twelve for approval of his ultimatum.

Number Three nodded his grotesque and hideous head – he was so covered with long black hair that he more nearly resembled an orang outang than a human being. Number Twelve looked doubtful.

'I think Number Ten is right,' he said at last. 'We are not human. We have no souls. We are things. And while you, Bulan, are beautiful, yet you are as much a soulless thing as we – that much von Horn taught us well. So I believe that it would be better were we to keep forever from the sight of men. I do not much like the thought of living with these strange, hairy monsters, but we might find a place here in the jungle where we could live alone and in peace.'

'I do not want to live alone,' cried Number Three. 'I want a mate, and I see a beautiful one yonder now. I am going after her,' and with that he again started toward a female orang outang; but the lady bared her fangs and retreated before his advance.

'Even the beasts will have none of us,' cried Number Ten

angrily. 'Let us take them by force then,' and he started after Number Three.

'Come back!' shouted Bulan, leaping after the two deserters.

As he raised his voice there came an answering cry from a little distance ahead – a cry for help, and it was in the agonized tones of a woman's voice.

'I am coming!' shouted Bulan, and without another glance at his mutinous crew he sprang through the line of menacing orang outangs.

XII

PERFIDY

On the morning that Bulan set out with his three monsters
from the deserted long-house in which they had spent the night,
Professor Maxon's party was speeding up the river, constantly
buoyed with hope by the repeated reports of natives that the
white girl had been seen passing in a war prahu.

In translating this information to Professor Maxon, von
Horn habitually made it appear that the girl was in the hands
of Number Thirteen, or Bulan, as they had now come to call
him owing to the natives' constant use of that name in speak-
ing of the strange, and formidable white giant who had in-
vaded their land.

At the last long-house below the gorge, the head of which
had witnessed Virginia Maxon's escape from the clutches of
Ninaka and Barunda, the searching party was forced to stop
owing to a sudden attack of fever which had prostrated the
professor. Here they found a woman who had a strange tale to
relate of a remarkable sight she had witnessed that very
morning.

It seemed that she had been straining tapioca in a little
stream which flowed out of the jungle at the rear of the long-
house when her attention was attracted by the crashing of an
animal through the bushes a few yards above her. As she looked
she saw a huge *mias pappan* cross the stream, bearing in his
arms the dead, or unconscious form of a white-skinned girl
with golden hair.

Her description of the *mias pappan* was such as to half convince von Horn that she might have seen Number Three carrying Virginia Maxon, although he could not reconcile the idea
with the story that the two Dyaks had told him of losing all of
Bulan's monsters in the jungle.

Of course it was possible that they might have made their
way over land to this point, but it seemed scarcely credible –
and then, how could they have come into possession of Virginia Maxon, whom every report except this last agreed was

still in the hands of Ninaka and Barunda. There was always the possibility that the natives had lied to him, and the more he questioned the Dyak woman the more firmly convinced he became that this was the fact.

The outcome of it was that von Horn finally decided to make an attempt to follow the trail of the creature that the woman had seen, and with this plan in view persuaded Muda Saffir to arrange with the chief of the long-house at which they then were to furnish him with trackers and an escort of warriors, promising them some splendid heads should they be successful in overhauling Bulan and his pack.

Professor Maxon was too ill to accompany the expedition, and von Horn set out alone with his Dyak allies. For a time after they departed Sing Lee fretted and fidgeted upon the verandah of the long-house. He wholly distrusted von Horn, and from motives of his own finally decided to follow him. The trail of the party was plainly discernible, and the Chinaman had no difficulty in following them, so that they had gone no great way before he came within hearing distance of them. Always just far enough behind to be out of sight, he kept pace with the little column as it marched through the torrid heat of the morning, until a little after noon he was startled by the sudden cry of a woman in distress, and the answering shout of a man.

The voices came from a point in the jungle a little to his right and behind him, and without waiting for the column to return, or even to ascertain if they had heard the cries, Sing ran rapidly in the direction of the alarm. For a time he saw nothing, but was guided by the snapping of twigs and the rustling of bushes ahead, where the authors of the commotion were evidently moving swiftly through the jungle.

Presently a strange sight burst upon his astonished vision. It was the hideous Number Three in mad pursuit of a female orang outang, and an instant later he saw Number Twelve and Number Ten in battle with two males, while beyond he heard the voice of a man shouting encouragement to someone as he dashed through the jungle. It was in this last event that Sing's interest centered, for he was sure that he recognized the voice as that of Bulan, while the first cry for help which he had heard had been in a woman's voice, and Sing knew that it's author could be none other than Virginia Maxon.

Those whom he pursued were moving rapidly through the jungle which was now becoming more and more open, but the Chinaman was no mean runner, and it was not long before he drew within sight of the object of his pursuit.

His first glimpse was of Bulan, running swiftly between two huge bull orang outangs that snapped and tore at him as he bounded forward cutting and slashing at his foes with his heavy whip. Just in front of the trio was another bull bearing in his arms the unconscious form of Virginia Maxon who had fainted at the first response to her cry for help. Sing was armed with a heavy revolver but he dared not attempt to use it for fear that he might wound either Bulan or the girl, and so he was forced to remain but a passive spectator of what ensued.

Bulan, notwithstanding the running battle the two bulls were forcing upon him, was gaining steadily upon the fleeing orang outang that was handicapped by the weight of the fair captive he bore in his huge, hairy arms. As they came into a natural clearing in the jungle the fleeing bull glanced back to see his pursuer almost upon him, and with an angry roar turned to meet the charge.

In another instant Bulan and the three bulls were rolling and tumbling about the ground, a mass of flying fur and blood from which rose fierce and angry roars and growls, while Virginia Maxon lay quietly upon the sward where her captor had dropped her.

Sing was about to rush forward and pick her up, when he saw von Horn and his Dyaks leap into the clearing, to which they had been guided by the sounds of the chase and the encounter. The doctor halted at the sight that met his eyes – the prostrate form of the girl and the man battling with three large bulls.

Then he gathered up Virginia Maxon, and with a sign to his Dyaks, who were thoroughly frightened at the mere sight of the white giant of whom they had heard such terrible stories, turned and hastened back in the direction from which they had come, leaving the man to what seemed must be a speedy and horrible death.

Sing Lee was astounded at the perfidy of the act. To Bulan alone was due the entire credit of having rescued Professor Maxon's daughter, and yet in the very presence of his self-sacrificing loyalty and devotion von Horn had deserted him without making the least attempt to aid him. But the wrinkled old Chinaman was made of different metal, and had started forward to assist Bulan when a heavy hand suddenly fell upon his shoulder. Looking around he saw the hideous face of Number Ten snarling into his. The bloodshot eyes of the monster were flaming with rage. He had been torn and chewed by the bull with which he had fought, and though he had finally overcome and killed the beast, a female, which he had pursued had eluded him. In a frenzy of passion and blood lust aroused by his wounds, disappointment and the taste of warm blood which still smeared his lips and face, he had been seeking the female when he suddenly stumbled upon the hapless Sing.

With a roar he grasped the Chinaman as though to break him in two, but Sing was not at all inclined to give up his life without a struggle, and Number Ten was quick to learn that no mean muscles moved beneath that wrinkled, yellow hide.

There could, however, have been but one outcome to the unequal struggle had Sing not been armed with a revolver, though it was several seconds before he could bring it into play upon the great thing that shook and tossed him about as though he had been a rat in the mouth of a terrier. But suddenly there was the sharp report of a fire arm, and another of Professor Maxon's unhappy experiments sank back into the nothingness from which he had conjured it.

Then Sing turned his attention to Bulan and his three savage assailants, but, except for the dead body of a bull orang outang upon the spot where he had last seen the four struggling, there was no sign either of the white man or his antagonists; nor, though he listened attentively, could he catch the slightest sound within the jungle other than the rustling of the leaves and the raucous cries of the brilliant birds that flitted among the gorgeous blooms about him.

For half an hour he searched in every direction, but finally, fearing that he might become lost in the mazes of the unfamiliar forest he reluctantly turned his face toward the river and the long-house that sheltered his party.

Here he found Professor Maxon much improved – the safe return of Virginia having acted as a tonic upon him. The girl and her father sat with von Horn upon the verandah of the long-house as Sing clambered up the notched log that led to it from the ground. At sight of Sing's wrinkled old face Virginia Maxon sprang to her feet and ran forward to greet him, for she had been very fond of the shrewd and kindly Chinaman of whom she had seen so much during the dreary months of her imprisonment within the campong.

'Oh, Sing,' she cried, 'where have you been? We were all so worried to think that no sooner was one of us rescued than another became lost.'

'Sing takee walk, Linee, las all,' said the grinning Chinaman. 'Velly glad see Linee black 'gain,' and that was all that Sing Lee had to say of the adventures through which he had just passed, and the strange sights that he had seen.

Again and again the girl and von Horn narrated the stirring scenes of the day, the latter being compelled to repeat all that had transpired from the moment that he had heard Virginia's cry, though it was apparent that he only consented to speak of his part in her rescue under the most considerable urging. Very pretty modesty, thought Sing when he had heard the doctor's version of the affair.

'You see,' said von Horn, 'when I reached the spot Number Three, the brute that you thought was an ape, had just turned you over to Number Thirteen, or, as the natives now call him, Bulan. You were then in a faint, and when I attacked Bulan he dropped you to defend himself. I had expected a bitter fight from him after the wild tales the natives had been telling of his ferocity, but it was soon evident that he is an arrant coward, for I did not even have to fire my revolver – a few thumps with the butt of it upon his brainless skull sent him howling into the jungle with his pack at his heels.'

'How fortunate it is, my dear doctor,' said Professor Maxon, 'that you were bright enough to think of trailing the miscreant into the jungle. But for that Virginia would still be in his clutches and by this time he would have been beyond all hope of capture. How can we ever repay you, dear friend?'

'That you were generous enough to arrange when we first embarked upon the search for your daughter,' replied von Horn.

'Just so, just so,' said the professor, but a shade of trouble tinged the expression of his face, and a moment later he arose, saying that he felt weak and tired and would go to his sleeping room and lie down for a while. The fact was that Professor Maxon regretted the promise he had made von Horn relative to his daughter.

Once before he had made plans for her marriage only to regret them later; he hoped that he had made no mistake this time, but he realized that it had scarcely been fair to Virginia to promise her to his assistant without first obtaining her consent. Yet a promise was a promise, and, again, was it not true that but for von Horn she would have been dead or worse than dead in a short time had she not been rescued from the clutches of the soulless Bulan? Thus did the old man justify his action, and clinch the determination that he had before reached to compel Virginia to wed von Horn should she, from some incomprehensible motive, demur. Yet he hoped that the girl would make it easy, by accepting voluntarily the man who had saved her life.

Left alone, or as he thought alone, with the girl in the growing shadows of the evening, von Horn thought the moment propitious for renewing his suit. He did not consider the natives squatting about them as of sufficient consequence to consider, since they would not understand the language in which he addressed Virginia, and in the dusk he failed to note that Sing squatted with the Dyaks, close behind them.

'Virginia,' he commenced, after an interval of silence, 'often before have I broached the subject nearest to my heart, yet never have you given me much encouragement. Can you not feel for the man who would gladly give his life for you, sufficient affection to permit you to make him the happiest man in the world? I do not ask for all your love at first – that will come later. Just give me the right to cherish and protect you. Say that you will be my wife, Virginia, and we need have no more fears that the strange vagaries of your father's mind can ever again jeopardize your life or your happiness as they have in the past.'

'I feel that I owe you my life,' replied the girl in a quiet voice, 'and while I am now positive that my father has entirely regained his sanity, and looks with as great abhorrence upon the terrible fate he planned for me as I myself, I cannot forget the debt of gratitude which belongs to you.

'At the same time I do not wish to be the means of making you unhappy, as surely would be the result were I to marry you without love. Let us wait until I know myself better. Though you have spoken to me of the matter before, I realize now that I never made any effort to determine whether or not I really can love you. There is time enough before we reach civilization, if ever we are fortunate enough to do so at all. Will you not be as generous as you are brave, and give me a few days before I must make you a final answer.'

With Professor Maxon's solemn promise to insure his ultimate success von Horn was very gentle and gracious in deferring to the girl's wishes. The girl for her part could not put from her mind the disappointment she had felt when she discovered that her rescuer was von Horn, and not the handsome young giant whom she had been positive was in close pursuit of her abductors.

When Number Thirteen had been mentioned she had always pictured him as a hideous monster, similar to the creature that had seized her in the jungle beside the encampment that first day she had seen the mysterious stranger, of whom she could obtain no information either from her father or von Horn. When she had recently insisted that the same man had been at the head of her father's creatures in an attempt to rescue her, both von Horn and Professor Maxon scoffed at the idea, until at last she was convinced that the fright and the firelight had conspired to conjure in her brain the likeness of one who was linked by memory to another time of danger and despair.

Virginia could not understand why it was that the face of the stranger persisted in obtruding itself in her memory. That the man was unusually good looking was undeniable, but she had known many good looking men, nor was she especially impressionable to mere superficial beauty. No words had passed between them on the occasion of their first meeting, so it could have been nothing that he said which caused the memory of him to cling so tenaciously in her mind.

What was it then? Was it the memory of the moments that she had lain in his strong arms – was it the shadow of the sweet, warm glow that had suffused her as his eyes had caught hers upon his face?

The thing was tantalizing – it was annoying. The girl blushed in mortification at the very thought that she could cling so resolutely to the memory of a total stranger, and – still greater humiliation – long in the secret depths of her soul to see him again.

She was angry with herself, but the more she tried to forget the young giant who had come into her life for so brief an instant, the more her mind persisted in dwelling upon him; and the more she speculated upon his identity and the strange fate that had brought him to their little, savage island only to snatch him away again as mysteriously as he had come, the less was the approval with which she looked upon the suit of Doctor von Horn.

Von Horn had left her, and strolled down to the river. Finally Virginia arose to seek the crude couch which had been spread for her in one of the sleeping rooms of the long-house. As she passed a group of natives squatted nearby one of the number arose and approached her, and as she halted, half in fright, a low voice whispered:

'Lookee out Linee, dloctor Hornee velly bad man.'

'Why Sing!' exclaimed Virginia. 'What in the world do you mean by saying such a thing as that?'

'Never mind, Linee; you always good to old Sing. Sing no likee see you sadee. Dloctor Hornee velly bad man, las allee,' and without another word the Chinaman turned and walked away.

XIII

BURIED TREASURE

After the escape of the girl Barunda and Ninaka had fallen out over that affair and the division of the treasure, with the result that the panglima had slipped a knife between the ribs of his companion and dropped the body overboard.

Barunda's followers, however, had been highly enraged at the act, and in the ensuing battle which they waged for revenge of their murdered chief Ninaka and his crew had been forced to take to the shore and hide in the jungle.

With difficulty they had saved the chest and dragged it after them into the mazes of the underbrush. Finally, however, they succeeded in eluding the angry enemy, and took up their march through the interior for the head of a river which would lead them to the sea by another route, it being Ninaka's intention to dispose of the contents of the chest as quickly as possible through the assistance of a rascally Malay who dwelt at Gunung Tebor, where he carried on a thieving trade with pirates.

But presently it became apparent that he had not so easily escaped the fruits of his villainy as he had supposed, for upon the evening of the first day the rear of his little column was attacked by some of Barunda's warriors who had forged ahead of their fellows, with the result that the head of Ninaka's brother went to increase the prestige and glory of the house of the enemy.

Ninaka was panic-stricken, since he knew that hampered as he was by the heavy chest he could neither fight nor run to advantage. And so, upon a dark night near the head waters of the river he sought, he buried the treasure at the foot of a mighty buttress tree, and with his parang made certain cabalistic signs upon the bole whereby he might identify the spot when it was safe to return and disinter his booty. Then, with his men, he hastened down the stream until they reached the head of prahu navigation where they stole a craft and paddled swiftly on towards the sea.

When the three bull orang outangs closed upon Bulan he

felt no fear as to the outcome of the battle, for never in his experience had he coped with any muscles that his own mighty thews could not overcome. But as the battle continued he realized that there might be a limit to the number of antagonists which he could successfully withstand, since he could scarcely hope with but two hands to reach the throats of three enemies, or ward off the blows and clutches of six powerful hands, or the gnashing of three sets of savage fangs.

When the truth dawned upon him that he was being killed the instinct of self-preservation was born in him. The ferocity with which he had fought before paled into insignificance beside the mad fury with which he now attacked the three terrible creatures upon him. Shaking himself like a great lion he freed his arms for a moment from the clinging embrace of his foemen, and seizing the neck of the nearest in his mighty clutch wrenched the head completely around.

There was one awful shriek from the tortured brute – the vertebrae parted with a snap, and Bulan's antagonists were reduced to two. Lunging and struggling the three combatants stumbled farther and farther into the jungle beyond the clearing. With mighty blows the man buffeted the beasts to right and left, but ever they returned in bestial rage to renew the encounter. Bulan was weakening rapidly under the terrific strain to which he had been subjected, and from loss of blood which flowed from his wounds; yet he was slowly mastering the foaming brutes, who themselves were torn and bleeding and exhausted. Weaker and weaker became the struggles of them all, when a sudden misstep sent Bulan stumbling headforemost against the stem of a tree, where, stunned, he sank unconscious, at the mercy of the relentless bulls.

They had already sprung upon the prostrate form of their victim to finish what the accident had commenced, when the loud report of Sing's revolver smote upon their startled ears as the Chinaman's bullet buried itself in the heart of Number Ten. Never had the orang outangs heard the sound of a firearm, and the noise, seemingly in such close proximity, filled them with such terror that on the instant they forgot all else than this new and startling fear, and with headlong haste leaped away into the jungle, leaving Bulan lying where he had fallen.

So it was that though Sing passed within a few paces of the

unconscious man he neither saw nor heard aught of him or his antagonists.

When Bulan returned to consciousness the day was drawing to a close. He was stiff and sore and weak. His head ached horribly. He thought that he must indeed be dying, for how could one who suffered so revive? But at last he managed to stagger to his feet, and finally to reach the stream along which he had been travelling earlier in the day. Here he quenched his thirst and bathed his wounds, and as darkness came he lay down to sleep upon a bed of matted grasses.

The next morning found him refreshed and in considerably less pain, for the powers of recuperation which belonged to his perfect health and mighty physique had already worked an almost miraculous transformation in him. While he was hunting in the jungle for his breakfast he came suddenly upon Number Three and Number Twelve similarly employed.

At sight of him the two creatures started to run away, but he called to them reassuringly and they returned. On closer inspection Bulan saw that both were covered with terrible wounds and after questioning them learned that they had fared almost as badly at the hands of the orang outangs as had he.

'Even the beasts loathe us,' exclaimed Number Twelve. 'What are we to do?'

'Leave the beasts alone, as I told you,' replied Bulan.

'Human beings hate us also,' persisted Number Twelve.

'Then let us live by ourselves,' suggested Number Three.

'We hate each other,' retorted the pessimistic Number Twelve. 'There is no place for us in the world, and no companionship. We are but soulless things.'

'Stop!' cried Bulan. 'I am not a soulless thing. I am a man, and within me is as fine and pure a soul as any man may own,' and to his mind's eye came the vision of a fair face surmounted by a mass of loosely waving, golden hair; but the brainless ones could not understand and only shook their heads as they resumed their feeding and forgot the subject.

When the three had satisfied the cravings of their appetites two of them were for lying down to sleep until it should be time to feed again, but Bulan, once more master, would not permit it, and forced them to accompany him in his seemingly futile search for the girl who had disappeared so mysteriously after he had rescued her from the orang outangs.

Both Number Twelve and Number Three had assured him that the beasts had not recaptured her, for they had seen the entire band flee madly through the jungle after hearing the report of the single shot which had so terrorized Bulan's antagonists. Bulan did not know what to make of this occurrence which he had not himself heard, the shot having come after he had lost consciousness at the foot of the tree; but from the description of the noise given him by Number Twelve he felt sure that it must have been the report of a gun, and hoped that it betokened the presence of Virginia Maxon's friends, and that she was now safe in their keeping.

Nevertheless he did not relinquish his determination to continue his search for her, since it was quite possible that the gun had been fired by a native, many of whom possessed firearms. His first concern was for the girl's welfare, which spoke eloquently for the chivalry of his character, and though he wished to see her for the pleasure that it would give him, the hope of serving her was ever the first consideration in his mind.

He was now confident that he was following the wrong direction, and with the intention in view of discovering the tracks of the party which had rescued or captured Virginia after he had been forced to relinquish her, he set out in a totally new direction away from the river. His small woodcraft and little experience in travelling resulted in his becoming completely confused, so that instead of returning to the spot where he had last seen the girl, as he wished to do, he bore far to the northeast of the place, and missed entirely the path which von Horn and his Dyaks had taken from the long-house into the jungle and return.

All that day he urged his reluctant companions on through the fearful heat of the tropics until, almost exhausted, they halted at dusk upon the bank of a river, where they filled their stomachs with cooling draughts, and after eating lay down to sleep. It was quite dark when Bulan was aroused by the sound of something approaching from up the river, and as he lay listening he presently heard the subdued voices of men conversing in whispers. He recognized the language as that of the Dyaks, though he could interpret nothing which they said.

Presently he saw a dozen warriors emerge into a little patch of moonlight. They bore a huge chest among them which they deposited within a few paces of where Bulan lay. Then they

commenced to dig in the soft earth with their spears and parangs until they had excavated a shallow pit. Into this they
lowered the chest, covering it over with earth and sprinkling
dead grass, twigs and leaves above it, that it might present to
a searcher no sign that the ground had recently been disturbed.
The balance of the loose earth which would not go back into
the pit was thrown into the river.

When all had been made to appear as it was before, one of
the warriors made several cuts and scratches upon the stem of
a tree which grew above the spot where the chest was buried;
then they hastened on in silence past Bulan and down the
river.

As von Horn stood by the river's bank after his conversation
with Virginia, he saw a small sampan approaching from up
stream. In it he made out two natives, and the stealthiness of
their approach caused him to withdraw into the shadow of a
large prahu which was beached close to where he had been
standing.

When the men had come close to the landing one of them
gave a low signal, and presently a native come down from the
long-house.

'Who is it comes by night?' he asked. 'And what want you?'

'News has just reached us that Muda Saffir is alive,' replied
one of the men in the boat, 'and that he sleeps this night in your
long-house. Is it true?'

'Yes,' answered the man on shore. 'What do you wish of the
Rajah Muda Saffir?'

'We are men of his company and we have news for him,'
returned the speaker in the sampan. 'Tell him that we must
speak to him at once.'

The native on shore returned to the long-house without
replying. Von Horn wondered what the important news for
Muda Saffir might be, and so he remained as he had been, concealed behind the prahu.

Presently the old Malay come down to the water's edge —
very warily though — and asked the men whom they might be.
When they had given their names he seemed relieved.

'Ninaka,' they said, 'has murdered Barunda who was taking
the rajah's treasure up to the rajah's stronghold — the treasure
which Ninaka had stolen after trying to murder the rajah and
which Barunda had recaptured. Now Ninaka, after murdering

Barunda, set off through the jungle toward the river which leads to Gunung Tebor, and Barunda's uncle followed him with what few men he had with him; but he sent us down river to try and find you, master, and beg of you to come with many men and overtake Ninaka and punish him.'

Muda Saffir thought for a moment.

'Hasten back to the uncle of Barunda and tell him that as soon as I can gather the warriors I shall come and punish Ninaka. I have another treasure here which I must not lose, but I can arrange that it will still be here when I return for it, and then Barunda's uncle can come back with me to assist me if assistance is needed. Also, be sure to tell Barunda's uncle never to lose sight of the treasure,' and Muda Saffir turned and hastened back to the long-house.

As the men in the sampan headed the boat's bow up stream again, von Horn ran along the jungle trail beside the river and abreast of the paddlers. When he thought that they were out of hearing of the long-house he hailed the two. In startled surprise the men ceased paddling.

'Who are you and what do you want?' asked one.

'I am the man to whom the chest belongs,' replied von Horn. 'If you will take me to Barunda's uncle before Muda Saffir reaches him you shall each have the finest rifles that the white man makes, with ammunition enough to last you a year. All I ask is that you guide me within sight of the party that pursues Ninaka; then you may leave me and tell no one what you have done, nor will I tell any. What say you?'

The two natives consulted together in low tones. At last they drew nearer the shore.

'Will you give us each a bracelet of brass as well as the rifles?' asked the spokesman.

Von Horn hesitated. He knew the native nature well. To have acquiesced too readily would have been to have invited still further demands from them.

'Only the rifles and ammunition,' he said at last, 'unless you succeed in keeping the knowledge of my presence from both Barunda's uncle and Muda Saffir. If you do that you shall have the bracelets also.'

The prow of the sampan touched the bank.

'Come!' said one of the warriors.

Von Horn stepped aboard. He was armed only with a brace

of Colts, and he was going into the heart of the wild country of the head hunters, to pit his wits against those of the wily Muda Saffir. His guides were two savage head hunting warriors of a pirate crew from whom he hoped to steal what they considered a fabulously rich treasure. Whatever sins might be laid to the door of the doctor, there could be no question but that he was a very brave man!

Von Horn's rash adventure had been suggested by the hope that he might, by bribing some of the natives with Barunda's uncle, make away with the treasure before Muda Saffir arrived to claim it, or, failing that, learn its exact whereabouts that he might return for it with an adequate force later. That he was taking his life in his hands he well knew, but so great was the man's cupidity that he reckoned no risk too great for the acquirement of a fortune.

The two Dyaks, paddling in silence up the dark river, proceeded for nearly three hours before they drew in to the bank and dragged the sampan up into the bushes. Then they set out upon a narrow trail into the jungle. It so happened that after travelling for several miles they inadvertently took another path than that followed by the party under Barunda's uncle, so that they passed the latter without being aware of it, going nearly half a mile to the right of where the trailers camped a short distance from the bivouac of Ninaka.

In the dead of night Ninaka and his party had crawled away under the very noses of the avengers, taking the chest with them, and by chance von Horn and the two Dyaks cut back into the main trail along the river almost at the very point that Ninaka halted to bury the treasure.

And so it was that Bulan was not the only one who watched the hiding of the chest.

When Ninaka had disappeared down the river trail Bulan lay speculating upon the strange actions he had witnessed. He wondered why the men should dig a hole in the midst of the jungle to hide away the box which he had so often seen in Professor Maxon's workshop. It occurred to him that it might be well to remember just where the thing was buried, so that he could lead the professor to it should he ever see the old man again.

As he lay thus, half dozing, his attention was attracted by a

124

stealthy rustling in the bushes nearby, and as he watched he was dumbfounded to see von Horn creep out into the moonlight. A moment later the man was followed by two Dyaks. The three stood conversing in low tones, pointing repeatedly at the spot where the chest lay hidden. Bulan could understand but little of their conversation, but it was evident that von Horn was urging some proposition to which the warriors demurred.

Suddenly, without an instant's warning, von Horn drew his gun, wheeled, and fired pointblank, first at one of his companions, then at the other. Both men fell in their tracks, and scarcely had the pungent odor of the powder smoke reached Bulan's nostrils ere the white man had plunged into the jungle and disappeared.

Failing in his attempt to undermine the loyalty of the two Dyaks von Horn had chosen the only other way to keep the knowledge of the whereabouts of the chest from Barunda's uncle and Muda Saffir, and now his principle interest in life was to escape the vengeance of the head hunters and return to the long-house before his absence should be detected.

There he could form a party of natives and set out to regain the chest after Muda Saffir and Barunda's uncle had given up the quest. That suspicion should fall on him seemed scarcely credible since the only men who knew that he had left the long-house that night lay dead upon the very spot where the treasure reposed.

As von Horn dropped swiftly down the river in the same sampan that had brought him up he passed two large war prahus forging rapidly up the stream. The man smiled as he realized that the boats contained Muda Saffir and his party hastening to recover the treasure. Had he known what else one of them contained he would not have smiled.

XIV

MAN OR MONSTER?

When Muda Saffir turned from the two Dyaks who had brought him news of the treasure he hastened to the long-house and arousing the chief of the tribe who domiciled there explained that necessity required that the rajah have at once two war prahus fully manned. Now the power of the crafty old Malay extended from one end of this great river on which the long-house lay to the other, and though not all the tribes admitted allegiance to him, yet there were few who would not furnish him with men and boats when he required them; for his piratical cruises carried him often up and down the stream, and with his savage horde it was possible for him to wreak summary and terrible vengeance upon those who opposed him.

When he had explained his wishes to the chief, the latter, though at heart hating and fearing Muda Saffir, dared not refuse; but to a second proposition he offered strong opposition until the rajah threatened to wipe out his entire tribe should he not accede to his demands.

The thing which the chief demurred to had occurred to Muda Saffir even as he walked back from the river after conversing with the two Dyaks messengers. The thought of regaining the treasure, the while he administered punishment to the traitorous Ninaka, filled his soul with savage happiness. Now if he could but once more possess himself of the girl! And why not? There was only the sick old man, a Chinaman and von Horn to prevent it, and the chances were that they all were asleep.

So he explained to the chief the plan that had so suddenly sprung to his wicked mind.

'Three men with parangs may easily quiet the old man, his assistant and the Chinaman,' he said, 'and then we can take the girl along with us.'

The chief refused at first, point-blank, to be a party to any such proceedings. He knew what had happened to the Sakkaran Dyaks after they had murdered a party of Englishmen, and he did not purpose laying himself and his tribe open to the vengeance of the white men who came in many boats and with countless guns and cannon to take a terrible toll for every drop of white blood spilled.

So it was that Muda Saffir was forced to compromise, and be satisfied with the chief's assistance in abducting the girl, for it was not so difficult a matter to convince the head hunter that she really belonged to the rajah, and that she had been stolen from him by the old man and the doctor.

Virginia slept in a room with three Dyak women. It was to this apartment that the chief finally consented to dispatch two of his warriors. The men crept noiselessly within the pitch dark interior until they came to the sleeping form of one of the Dyak woman. Cautiously they awoke her.

'Where is the white girl?' asked one of the men in a low whisper. 'Muda Saffir has sent us for her. Tell her that her father is very sick and wants her, but do not mention Muda Saffir's name lest she might not come.'

The whispering awakened Virginia and she lay wondering what the cause of the midnight conference might be, for she recognized that one of the speakers was a man, and there had been no man in the apartment when she had gone to sleep earlier in the night.

Presently she heard some one approach her, and a moment later a woman's voice addressed her; but she could not understand enough of the native tongue to make out precisely the message the speaker wished to convey. The words 'father', 'sick' and 'come', however she finally understood after several repetitions, for she had picked up a smattering of the Dyak language during her enforced association with the natives.

The moment that the possibilities suggested by these few words dawned upon her, she sprang to her feet and followed the woman toward the door of the apartment. Immediately without, the two warriors stood upon the verandah awaiting their victim, and as Virginia passed through the doorway she was seized roughly from either side, a heavy hand was clapped over her mouth, and before she could make even an effort to rebel she had been dragged to the end of the verandah, down the notched log to the ground and a moment later found herself in a war prahu which was immediately pushed into the stream.

Since Virginia had come to the long-house after her rescue from the ourang outangs, supposedly by von Horn, Rajah Muda Saffir had kept very much out of sight, for he knew that should the girl see him she would recognize him as the man who had stolen her from the Ithaca. So it came as a mighty shock to the girl when she heard the hated tones of the man whom she had knocked overboard from the prahu two nights before, and realized that the bestial Malay sat close beside her, and that she was again in his power. She looked now for no mercy, nor could she hope to again escape him so easily as she had before, and so she sat with bowed head in the bottom of the swiftly moving craft, buried in anguished thoughts, hopeless and miserable.

Along the stretch of black river that the prahu and her consort covered that night Virginia Maxon saw no living thing other than a single figure in a small sampan which hugged the shadows of the shore as the two larger boats met and passed it, nor answered their hail.

Where von Horn and his two Dyak guides had landed, Muda Saffir's force disembarked and plunged into the jungle. Rapidly they hastened along the well known trail toward the point designated by the two messengers, to come upon the spot simultaneously with the party under Barunda's uncle, who, startled by the two shots several hours previously, had been cautiously searching through the jungle for an explanation of them.

They had gone warily for fear that they might stumble upon Ninaka's party before Muda Saffir arrived with reinforcements, and but just now had they discovered the prostrate forms of their two companions. One was dead, but the other was still conscious and had just sufficient vitality left after the coming of his fellows to whisper that they had been treacherously shot by the younger white man who had been at the long-house where they had found Muda Saffir – then the fellow expired without having an opportunity to divulge the secret hiding place of the treasure, over the top of which his body lay.

Now Bulan had been an interested witness of all that transpired. At first he had been inclined to come out of his hiding place and follow von Horn, but so much had already occurred beneath the branches of the great tree where the chest lay hidden that he decided to wait until morning at least, for he was sure that he had by no means seen the last of the drama which surrounded the heavy box. This belief was strengthened by the haste displayed by both Ninaka and von Horn to escape the neighborhood as quickly as possible, as though they feared that they might be apprehended should they delay for a moment.

Number Three and Number Twelve still slept, not having been aroused even by the shots fired by von Horn. Bulan himself had dozed after the departure of the doctor, but the advent of Barunda's uncle with his followers had awakened him, and now he lay wide eyed and alert as the second party, under Muda Saffir, came into view when they left the jungle trail and entered the clearing.

His interest in either party was but passive until he saw the khaki blouse, short skirt and trim leggings of the captive walking between two of the Dyaks of Muda Saffir's company. At the same instant he recognized the evil features of the rajah as those of the man who had directed the abduction of Virginia Maxon from the wrecked Ithaca.

Like a great cat Bulan drew himself cautiously to all fours – every nerve and muscle taut with the excitement of the moment. Before him he saw a hundred and fifty ferocious Borneo head hunters, armed with parangs, spears and sumpitans. At his back slept two almost brainless creatures – his sole support against the awful odds he must face before he could hope to succor the divinity whose image was enshrined in his brave and simple heart.

The muscles stood out upon his giant forearm as he gripped the stock of his bull whip. He believed that he was going to his death, for mighty as were his thews he knew that in the face of the horde they would avail him little, yet he saw no other way than to sit supinely by while the girl went to her doom, and that he could not do. He nudged Number Twelve. 'Silence!' he whispered, and, 'Come! The girl is here. We must save her. Kill the men,' and the same to the hairy and terrible Number Three.

Both the creatures awoke and rose to their hands and knees without noise that could be heard above the chattering of the natives, who had crowded forward to view the dead bodies of von Horn's victims. Silently Bulan came to his feet, the two monsters at his back rising and pressing close behind him. Along the denser shadows the three crept to a position in the rear of the natives. The girl's guards had stepped forward with the others to join in the discussion that followed the dying statement of the murdered warrior, leaving her upon the outer fringe of the crowd.

For an instant a sudden hope of escape sprang to Virginia Maxon's mind – there was none between her and the jungle through which they had just passed. Though unknown dangers lurked in the black and uncanny depths of the dismal forest, would not death in any form be far preferable to the hideous fate which awaited her in the person of the bestial Malay pirate?

She had turned to take the first step toward freedom when three figures emerged from the wall of darkness behind her. She saw the war-caps, shields, and war-coats, and her heart sank. Here were others of the rajah's party – stragglers who had come just in time to thwart her plans. How large these men were – she never had seen a native of such giant proportions; and now they had come quite close to her, and as the foremost stooped to speak to her she shrank back in fear. Then, to her surprise, she heard in whispered English; 'Come quietly, while they are not looking.'

She thought the voice familiar, but could not place it, though her heart whispered that it might belong to the young stranger of her dreams. He reached out and took her hand and together they turned and walked quickly toward the jungle, followed by the two who had accompanied him.

Scarcely had they covered half the distance before one of the Dyaks whose duty it had been to guard the girl discovered that she was gone. With a cry he alarmed his fellows, and in another instant a sharp pair of eyes caught the movement of the four who had now broken into a run.

With savage shouts the entire force of head hunters sprang in pursuit. Bulan lifted Virginia in his arms and dashed on ahead of Number Twelve and Number Three. A shower of poisoned darts blown from half a hundred sumpitans fell about them, and then Muda Saffir called to his warriors to cease using their deadly blow-pipes lest they kill the girl.

Into the jungle dashed the four while close behind them came the howling pack of enraged savages. Now one closed upon Number Three only to fall back dead with a broken neck as the giant fingers released their hold upon him. A parang swung close to Number Twelve, but his own, which he had now learned to wield with fearful effect, clove through the pursuing warrior's skull splitting him wide to the breast bone.

Thus they fought the while they forced their way deeper and deeper into the dark mazes of the entangled vegetation. The brunt of the running battle was borne by the two monsters, for Bulan was carrying Virginia, and keeping a little ahead of his companions to insure the girl's greater safety.

Now and then patches of moonlight filtering through occasional openings in the leafy roofing revealed to Virginia the battle that was being waged for possession of her, and once, when Number Three turned toward her after disposing of a new assailant, she was horrified to see the grotesque and terrible face of the creature. A moment later she caught sight of Number Twelve's hideous face. She was appalled.

Could it be that she had been rescued from the Malay to fall into the hands of creatures equally heartless and entirely without souls? She glanced up at the face of him who carried her. In the darkness of the night she had not yet had an opportunity to see the features of the man, but after a glimpse at those of his two companions she trembled to think of the hideous thing that might be revealed to her.

Could it be that she had at last fallen into the hands of the dreaded and terrible Number Thirteen! Instinctively she shrank from contact with the man in whose arms she had been carried without a trace of repugnance until the thought obtruded itself that he might be the creature of her father's mad experimentation, to whose arms she had been doomed by the insane obsession of her parent.

The man shifted her now to give himself freer use of his right arm, for the savages were pressing more closely upon Twelve and Three, and the change made it impossible for the girl to see his face even in the more frequent moonlit places.

But she could see the two who ran and fought just behind them, and she shuddered at her inevitable fate. For should the three be successful in bearing her away from the Dyaks she must face an unknown doom, while should the natives recapture her there was the terrible Malay into whose clutches she had already twice fallen.

Now the head hunters were pressing closer, and suddenly, even as the girl looked directly at him, a spear passed through the heart of Number Three. Clutching madly at the shaft protruding from his misshapen body the grotesque thing stumbled on for a dozen paces, and then sank to the ground as two of the brown warriors sprang upon him with naked parangs. An instant later Virginia Maxon saw the hideous and grisly head swinging high in the hand of a dancing, whooping savage.

The man who carried her was now forced to turn and fight off the enemy that pressed forward past Number Twelve. The mighty bull whip whirled and cracked across the heads and faces of the Dyaks. It was a formidable weapon when backed by the Herculean muscles that rolled and shifted beneath Bulan's sun-tanned skin, and many were the brown warriors that went down beneath its cruel lash.

Virginia could see that the creature who bore her was not deformed of body, but she shrank from the thought of what a sight of his face might reveal. How much longer the two could fight off the horde at their heels the girl could not guess; and as a matter of fact she was indifferent to the outcome of the strange, running battle that was being waged with herself as the victor's spoil.

The country was now becoming rougher and more open. The flight seemed to be leading into a range of low hills, where the jungle grew less dense, and the way rocky and rugged. They had entered a narrow cañon when Number Twelve went down beneath a half dozen parangs. Again the girl saw a bloody head swung on high and heard the fierce, wild chorus of exulting victory. She wondered how long it would be ere the creature beneath her would add his share to the grim trophies of the hunt.

In the interval that the head hunters had paused to sever Number Twelve's head, Bulan had gained fifty yards upon them, and then, of a sudden, he came to a sheer wall rising straight across the narrow trail he had been following. Ahead there was no way – a cat could scarce have scaled that formidable barrier – but to the right he discerned what appeared to be a steep and winding pathway up the cañon's side, and with a bound he clambered along it to where it surmounted the rocky wall.

There he turned, winded, to await the oncoming foe. Here was a spot where a single man might defy an army, and Bulan had been quick to see the natural advantages of it. He placed the girl upon her feet behind a protruding shoulder of the cañon's wall which rose to a considerable distance still above them. Then he turned to face the mob that was surging up the narrow pathway toward him.

At his feet lay an accumulation of broken rock from the hillside above, and as a spear sped, singing, close above his shoulder, the occurrence suggested a use for the rough and jagged missiles which lay about him in such profusion. Many of the pieces were large, weighing twenty and thirty pounds, and some even as much as fifty. Picking up one of the larger Bulan raised it high above his head, and then hurled it down amongst the upclimbing warriors. In an instant pandemonium reigned, for the heavy boulder had mowed down a score of the pursuers, breaking arms and legs in its meteoric descent.

Missile after missile Bulan rained down upon the struggling, howling Dyaks, until, seized by panic, they turned and fled incontinently down into the depths of the cañon and back along the narrow trail they had come, and then superstitious fear completed the rout that the flying rocks had started, for one whispered to another that this was the terrible Bulan and that he had but lured them on into the hills that he might call forth all his demons and destroy them.

For a moment Bulan stood watching the retreating savages, a smile upon his lips, and then as the sudden equatorial dawn burst forth he turned to face the girl.

As Virginia Maxon saw the fine features of the giant where she had expected to find the grotesque and hideous lineaments of a monster, she gave a quick little cry of pleasure and relief.

'Thank God!' she cried fervently. 'Thank God that you are a man – I thought that I was in the clutches of the hideous and soulless monster, Number Thirteen.'

The smile upon the young man's face died. An expression of pain, and hopelessness, and sorrow swept across his features. The girl saw the change, and wondered, but how could she guess the grievous wound her words had inflicted.

XV

TOO LATE

For a moment the two stood in silence; Bulan tortured by thoughts of the bitter humiliation that he must suffer when the girl should learn his identity; Virginia wondering at the sad lines that had come into the young man's face, and at his silence.

It was the girl who spoke first. 'Who are you,' she asked, 'to whom I owe my safety?'

The man hesitated. To speak aught than the truth had never occurred to him during his brief existence. He scarcely knew how to lie. To him a question demanded but one manner of reply – the facts. But never before had he had to face a question where so much depended upon his answer. He tried to form the bitter, galling words; but a vision of that lovely face suddenly transformed with horror and disgust throttled the name in his throat.

'I am Bulan,' he said, at last, quietly.

'Bulan,' repeated the girl. 'Bulan. Why that is a native name. You are either an Englishman or an American. What is your true name?'

'My name is Bulan,' he insisted doggedly.

Virginia Maxon thought that he must have some good reason of his own for wishing to conceal his identity. At first she wondered if he could be a fugitive from justice – the perpetrator of some horrid crime, who dared not divulge his true name even in the remote fastness of a Bornean wilderness; but a glance at his frank and noble countenance drove every vestige of the traitorous thought from her mind. Her woman's intuition was sufficient guarantee of the nobility of his character.

'Then let me thank you, Mr. Bulan,' she said, 'for the service that you have rendered a strange and helpless woman.'

He smiled.

'Just Bulan,' he said. 'There is no need for Miss or Mister in the savage jungle, Virginia.'

The girl flushed at the sudden and unexpected use of her given name, and was surprised that she was not offended.

'How do you know my name?' she asked.

Bulan saw that he would get into deep water if he attempted to explain too much, and, as is ever the way, discovered that one deception had led him into another; so he determined to forestall future embarrassing queries by concocting a story immediately to explain his presence and his knowledge.

'I lived upon the island near your father's camp,' he said. 'I knew you all – by sight.'

'How long have you lived there?' asked the girl. 'We thought the island was uninhabited.'

'All my life,' replied Bulan truthfully.

'It is strange,' she mused. 'I cannot understand it. But the monsters – how is it that they followed you and obeyed your commands?'

Bulan touched the bull whip that hung at his side.

'Von Horn taught them to obey this,' he said.

'He used that upon them?' cried the girl in horror.

'It was the only way,' said Bulan. 'They were almost brainless – they could understand nothing else, for they could not reason.'

Virginia shuddered.

'Where are they now – the balance of them?' she asked.

'They are dead, poor things,' he replied, sadly. 'Poor, hideous, unloved, unloving monsters – they gave up their lives for the daughter of the man who made them the awful, repulsive creatures that they were.'

'What do you mean?' cried the girl.

'I mean that all have been killed searching for you, and battling with your enemies. They were soulless creatures, but they loved the mean lives they gave up so bravely for you whose father was the author of their misery – you owe a great deal to them, Virginia.'

'Poor things,' murmured the girl, 'but yet they are better off, for without brains or souls there could be no happiness in life for them. My father did them a hideous wrong, but it was an unintentional wrong. His mind was crazed with dwelling upon the wonderful discovery he had made, and if he wronged them he contemplated a still more terrible wrong to be inflicted upon me, his daughter.'

'I do not understand,' said Bulan.

'It was his intention to give me in marriage to one of his

soulless monsters – to the one he called Number Thirteen. Oh, it is terrible even to think of the hideousness of it; but now they are all dead he cannot do it even though his poor mind, which seems well again, should suffer a relapse.'

'Why do you loathe them so?' asked Bulan. 'Is it because they are hideous, or because they are soulless?'

'Either fact were enough to make them repulsive,' replied the girl, 'but it is the fact that they were without souls that made them totally impossible – one easily overlooks physical deformity, but the moral depravity that must be inherent in a creature without a soul must forever cut him off from intercourse with human beings.'

'And you think that regardless of their physical appearance the fact that they were without souls would have been apparent?' asked Bulan.

'I am sure of it,' cried Virginia. 'I would know the moment I set my eyes upon a creature without a soul.'

With all the sorrow that was his, Bulan could scarce repress a smile, for it was quite evident either that it was impossible to perceive a soul, or else that he possessed one.

'Just how do you distinguish the possessor of a soul?' he asked. . .

The girl cast a quick glance up at him.

'You are making fun of me,' she said.

'Not at all,' he replied. 'I am just curious as to how souls make themselves apparent. I have seen men kill one another as beasts kill. I have seen one who was cruel to those within his power, yet they were all men with souls. I have seen eleven soulless monsters die to save the daughter of a man whom they believed had wronged them terribly – a man with a soul. How then am I to know what attributes denote the possession of the immortal spark? How am I to know whether or no I possess a soul?'

Virginia smiled.

'You are courageous and honorable and chivalrous – those are enough to warrant the belief that you have a soul, were it not apparent from your countenance that you are of the higher type of mankind,' she said.

'I hope that you will never change your opinion of me, Virginia,' said the man; but he knew that there lay before her a severe shock, and before him a great sorrow when they should come to where her father was and the girl should learn the truth concerning him.

That he did not himself tell her may be forgiven him, for he had only a life of misery to look forward to after she should know that he, too, was equally a soulless monster with the twelve that had preceded him to a merciful death. He would have envied them but for the anticipation of the time that he might be alone with her before she learned the truth.

As he pondered the future there came to him the thought that should they never find Professor Maxon or von Horn the girl need never know but that he was a human being. He need not lose her then, but always be near her. The idea grew and with it the mighty temptation to lead Virginia Maxon far into the jungle, and keep her forever from the sight of men. And why not? Had he not saved her where others had failed? Was she not, by all that was just and fair, his?

Did he owe any loyalty to either her father or von Horn? All ready he had saved Professor Maxon's life, so the obligation, if there was any, lay all against the older man; and three times he had saved Virginia. He would be very kind and good to her. She should be much happier and a thousand times safer than with those others who were so poorly equipped to protect her.

As he stood silently gazing out across the jungle beneath them toward the new sun the girl watched him in a spell of admiration of his strong and noble face, and his perfect physique. What would have been her emotions had she guessed what thoughts were his! It was she who broke the silence.

'Can you find the way to the long-house where my father is?' she asked.

Bulan, startled at the question, looked up from his reverie. The thing must be faced, then, sooner than he thought. How was he to tell her of his intention? It occurred to him to sound her first — possibly she would make no objection to the plan.

'You are anxious to return?' he asked.

'Why, yes, of course, I am,' she replied. 'My father will be half mad with apprehension, until he knows that I am safe. What a strange question, indeed.' Still, however, she did not doubt the motives of her companion.

'Suppose we should be unable to find our way to the long-house?' he continued.

138

'Oh, don't say such a thing,' cried the girl. 'It would be terrible. I should die of misery and fright and loneliness in this awful jungle. Surely you can find your way to the river – it was but a short march through the jungle from where we landed to the spot at which you took me away from that fearful Malay.'

The girl's words cast a cloud over Bulan's hopes. The future looked less roseate with the knowledge that she would be unhappy in the life that he had been mapping for them. He was silent – thinking. In his breast a riot of conflicting emotions were waging the first great battle which was to point the trend of the man's character – would the selfish and the base prevail, or would the noble?

With the thought of losing her his desire for her companionship became almost a mania. To return her to her father and von Horn would be to lose her – of that there could be no doubt, for they would not leave her long in ignorance of his origin. Then, in addition to being deprived of her forever, he must suffer the galling mortification of her scorn.

It was a great deal to ask of a fledgling morality that was yet scarcely cognizant of its untried wings; but even as the man wavered between right and wrong there crept into his mind the one great and burning question of his life – had he a soul? And he knew that upon his decision of the fate of Virginia Maxon rested to some extent the true answer to that question, for, unconsciously, he had worked out his own crude soul hypothesis which imparted to this invisible entity the power to direct his actions only for good. Therefore he reasoned that wickedness presupposed a small and worthless soul, or the entire lack of one.

That she would hate a soulless creature he accepted as a foregone conclusion. He desired her respect, and that fact helped him to his final decision, but the thing that decided him was born of the truly chivalrous nature he possessed – he wanted Virginia Maxon to be happy; it mattered not at what cost to him.

The girl had been watching him closely as he stood silently thinking after her last words. She did not know the struggle that the calm face hid; yet she felt that the dragging moments were big with the question of her fate.

'Well?' she said at length.

'We must eat first,' he replied in a matter-of-fact tone, and not at all as though he was about to renounce his life's happiness, 'and then we shall set out in search of your father. I shall take you to him, Virginia, if man can find him.'

'I knew that you could,' she said, simply, 'but how my father and I ever can repay you I do not know – do you?'

'Yes,' said Bulan, and there was a sudden rush of fire to his eyes that kept Virginia Maxon from urging a detailed explanation of just how she might repay him.

In truth she did not know whether to be angry, or frightened, or glad of the truth that she read there; or mortified that it had awakened in her a realization that possibly an analysis of her own interest in this young stranger might reveal more than she had imagined.

The constraint that suddenly fell upon them was relieved when Bulan motioned her to follow him back down the trail into the gorge in search of food. There they sat together upon a fallen tree beside a tiny rivulet, eating the fruit that the man gathered. Often their eyes met as they talked, but always the girl's fell before the open worship in the man's.

Many were the men who had looked in admiration at Virginia Maxon in the past, but never, she felt, with eyes so clean and brave and honest. There was no guile or evil in them, and because of it she wondered all the more that she could not face them.

'What a wonderful soul those eyes portray,' she thought, 'and how perfectly they assure the safety of my life and honor while their owner is near me.'

And the man thought: 'Would that I owned a soul that I might aspire to live always near her – always to protect her.'

When they had eaten the two set out once more in search of the river, and the confidence that is born of ignorance was theirs, so that beyond each succeeding tangled barrier of vines and creepers they looked to see the swirling stream that would lead them to the girl's father.

On and on they trudged, the man often carrying the girl across the rougher obstacles and through the little streams that crossed their path, until at last came noon, and yet no sign of the river they sought. The combined jungle craft of the two had been insufficient either to trace the way that they had come, or point the general direction of the river.

As the afternoon drew to a close Virginia Maxon commenced

to lose heart – she was confident that they were lost. Bulan made no pretence of knowing the way, the most that he would say being that eventually they must come to the river. As a matter-of-fact had it not been for the girl's evident concern he would have been glad to know that they were irretrievably lost; but for her sake his efforts to find the river were conscientious.

When at last night closed down upon them the girl was, at heart, terror stricken, but she hid her true state from the man, because she knew that their plight was no fault of his. The strange and uncanny noises of the jungle night filled her with the most dreadful forebodings, and when a cold, drizzling rain set in upon them her cup of misery was full.

Bulan rigged a rude shelter for her, making her lie down beneath it, and then he removed his Dyak war-coat and threw it over her, but it was hours before her exhausted body overpowered her nervous fright and won a fitful and restless slumber. Several times Virginia became obsessed with the idea that Bulan had left her alone there in the jungle, but when she called his name he answered from close beside her shelter.

She thought that he had reared another for himself nearby, but even the thought that he might sleep filled her with dread, yet she would not call to him again, since she knew that he needed his rest even more than she. And all the night Bulan stood close beside the woman he had learned to love – stood almost naked in the chill night air and the cold rain, lest some savage man or beast creep out of the darkness after her while he slept.

The next day with its night, and the next, and the next were but repetitions of the first. It had become an agony of suffering for the man to fight off sleep longer. The girl read part of the truth in his heavy eyes and worn face, and tried to force him to take needed rest, but she did not guess that he had not slept for four days and nights.

At last abused Nature succumbed to the terrific strain that had been put upon her, and the giant constitution of the man went down before the cold and the wet, weakened and impoverished by loss of sleep and insufficient food; for through the last two days he had been able to find but little, and that little he had given to the girl, telling her that he had eaten his fill while he gathered hers.

It was on the fifth morning, when Virginia awoke, that she

found Bulan rolling and tossing upon the wet ground before her shelter, delirious with fever. At the sight of the mighty figure reduced to pitiable inefficiency and weakness, despite the knowledge that her protector could no longer protect, the fear of the jungle faded from the heart of the young girl – she was no more a weak and trembling daughter of an effete civilization. Instead she was a lioness, watching over and protecting her sick mate. The analogy did not occur to her, but something else did as she saw the flushed face and fever wracked body of the man whose appeal to her she would have thought purely physical had she given the subject any analytic consideration; and as a realization of his utter helplessness came to her she bent over him and kissed first his forehead and then his lips.

'What a noble and unselfish love yours has been,' she murmured. 'You have even tried to hide it that my position might be the easier to bear, and now that it may be too late I learn that I love you – that I have always loved you. Oh, Bulan, my Bulan, what a cruel fate that permitted us to find one another only to die together!'

XVI

SING SPEAKS

For a week Professor Maxon with von Horn and Sing sought for Virginia. They could get no help from the natives of the long-house, who feared the vengeance of Muda Saffir should he learn that they had aided the white men upon his trail.

And always as the three hunted through the jungle and up and down the river there lurked ever near a handful of the men of the tribe of the two whom von Horn had murdered, waiting for the chance that would give them revenge and the heads of the three they followed. They feared the guns of the white men too much to venture an open attack, and at night the quarry never abated their watchfulness, so that days dragged on, and still the three continued their hopeless quest unconscious of the relentless foe that dogged their footsteps.

Von Horn was always searching for an opportunity to enlist the aid of the friendly natives in an effort to regain the chest, but so far he had found none who would agree to accompany him even in consideration of a large share of the booty. It was the treasure alone which kept him to the search for Virginia Maxon, and he made it a point to direct the hunt always in the vicinity of the spot where it was buried, for a great fear consumed him that Ninaka might return and claim it before he had a chance to make away with it.

Three times during the week they returned and slept at the long-house, hoping each time to learn that the natives had received some news of her they sought, through the wonderful channels of communication that seemed always open across the trackless jungle and up and down the savage, lonely rivers.

For two days Bulan lay raving in the delirium of fever, while the delicate girl, unused to hardship and exposure, watched over him and nursed him with the loving tenderness and care of a young mother with her first born.

For the most part the young giant's ravings were inarticulate, but now and then Virginia heard her name linked with words of reverence and worship. The man fought again the recent battles he had passed through, and again suffered the long night watches beside the sleeping girl who filled his heart. Then it was that she learned the truth of his self-sacrificing devotion. The thing that puzzled her most was the repetition of a number and a name which ran through all his delirium – 'Nine ninety nine Priscilla.'

She could make neither head nor tail of it, nor was there another word to give a clue to its meaning, so at last from constant repetition it became a commonplace and she gave it no further thought.

The girl had given up hope that Bulan ever could recover, so weak and emaciated had he become, and when the fever finally left him quite suddenly she was positive that it was the beginning of the end. It was on the morning of the seventh day since they had commenced their wandering in search of the long-house that, as she sat watching him, she saw his eyes resting upon her face with a look of recognition.

Gently she took his hand, and at the act he smiled up at her very weakly.

'You are better, Bulan,' she said. 'You have been very sick, but now you shall soon be well again.'

She did not believe her own words, yet the mere saying of them gave her renewed hope.

'Yes,' replied the man, 'I shall soon be well again. How long have I been like this?'

'For two days,' she replied.

'And you have watched over me alone in the jungle for two days?' he asked incredulously.

'Had it been for life,' she said in a low voice, 'it would scarce have repaid the debt I owe you.'

For a long time he lay looking up into her eyes – longingly, wistfully.

'I wish that it had been for life,' he said.

At first she did not quite realize what he meant, but presently the tired and hopeless expression of his eyes brought to her a sudden knowledge of his meaning.

'Oh, Bulan,' she cried, 'you must not say that. Why should you wish to die?'

'Because I love you, Virginia,' he replied. 'And because, when you know what I am, you will hate and loathe me.'

On the girl's lips was an avowal of her own love, but as she bent closer to whisper the words in his ear there came the sound of men crashing through the jungle, and as she turned to face the peril that she thought approaching, von Horn sprang into view, while directly behind him came her father and Sing Lee.

Bulan saw them at the same instant, and as Virginia ran forward to greet her father he staggered weakly to his feet. Von Horn was the first to see the young giant, and with an oath sprang toward him, drawing his revolver as he came.

'You beast,' he cried. 'We have caught you at last.'

At the words Virginia turned back toward Bulan with a little scream of warning and of horror. Professor Maxon was behind her.

'Shoot the monster, von Horn,' he ordered. 'Do not let him escape.'

Bulan drew himself to his full height, and though he wavered from weakness, yet he towered mighty and magnificent above the evil faced man who menaced him.

'Shoot!' he said calmly. 'Death cannot come too soon now.'

At the same instant von Horn pulled the trigger. The giant's head fell back, he staggered, whirled about, and crumpled to the earth just as Virginia Maxon's arms closed about him.

Von Horn rushed close and pushing the girl aside pressed the muzzle of his gun to Bulan's temple, but an avalanche of wrinkled, yellow skin was upon him before he could pull the trigger a second time, and Sing had hurled him back a dozen feet and snatched his weapon.

Moaning and sobbing Virginia threw herself upon the body of the man she loved, while Professor Maxon hurried to her side to drag her away from the soulless thing for whom he had once intended her.

Like a tigress the girl turned upon the two white men.

'You are murderers,' she cried. 'Cowardly murderers. Weak and exhausted by fever he could not combat you, and so you have robbed the world of one of the noblest men that God ever created.'

'Hush!' cried Professor Maxon. 'Hush, child, you do not know what you say. The thing was a monster — a soulless monster.'

At the words the girl looked up quickly at her father, a faint realization of his meaning striking her like a blow in the face.

'What do you mean?' she whispered. 'Who was he?'

It was von Horn who answered.

'No god created that,' he said, with a contemptuous glance at the still body of the man at their feet. 'He was one of the creatures of your father's mad experiments – the soulless thing for whose arms his insane obsession doomed you. The thing at your feet, Virginia, was Number Thirteen.'

With a piteous little moan the girl turned back toward the body of the young giant. A faltering step she took toward it, and then to the horror of her father she sank upon her knees beside it and lifting the man's head in her arms covered the face with kisses.

'Virginia!' cried the professor. 'Are you mad, child?'

'I am not mad,' she moaned, 'not yet. I love him. Man or monster, it would have been all the same to me, for I loved him.'

Her father turned away, burying his face in his hands.

'God!' he muttered. 'What an awful punishment you have visited upon me for the sin of the thing I did.'

The silence which followed was broken by Sing who had kneeled opposite Virginia upon the other side of Bulan, where he was feeling the giant's wrists and pressing his ear close above his heart.

'Do'n cly, Linee,' said the kindly old Chinaman. 'Him no dlead.' Then, as he poured a pinch of brownish powder into the man's mouth from a tiny sack he had brought forth from the depths of one of his sleeves: 'Him no mlonster either, Linee. Him white man, alsame Mlaxon. Sing know.'

The girl looked up at him in gratitude.

'He is not dead, Sing? He will live?' she cried. 'I don't care about anything else, Sing, if you will only make him live.'

'Him live. Gettem lilee flesh wounds. Las all.'

'What do you mean by saying that he is not a monster?' demanded von Horn.

'You waitee, you dam flool,' cried Sing. 'I tellee lot more I know. You waitee I flixee him, and then, by God, I flixee you.'

Von Horn took a menacing step toward the Chinaman, his face black with wrath, but Professor Maxon interposed.

'This has gone quite far enough, Doctor von Horn,' he said. 'It may be that we acted hastily. I do not know, of course, what Sing means, but I intend to find out. He has been very faithful to us, and deserves every consideration.'

Von Horn stepped back, still scowling. Sing poured a little water between Bulan's lips, and then asked Professor Maxon for his brandy flask. With the first few drops of the fiery liquid the giant's eyelids moved, and a moment later he raised them and looked about him.

The first face he saw was Virginia's. It was full of love and compassion.

'They have not told you yet?' he asked.

'Yes,' she replied. 'They have told me, but it makes no difference. You have given me the right to say it, Bulan, and I do say it now again, before them all – I love you, and that is all there is that makes any difference.'

A look of happiness lighted his face momentarily, only to fade as quickly as it had come.

'No, Virginia,' he said, sadly, 'it would not be right. It would be wicked. I am not a human being. I am only a soulless monster. You cannot mate with such as I. You must go away with your father. Soon you will forget me.'

'Never, Bulan!' cried the girl, determinedly.

The man was about to attempt to dissuade her, when Sing interrupted.

'You keepee still, Bulan,' he said. 'You wait till Sing tellee. You no mlonster. Mlaxon he no makee you. Sing he find you in low bloat jus' outsidee cove. You dummy. No know nothing. No know namee. No know where comee from. No talkee.

'Sing he jes' hearee Mlaxon tellee Hornee 'bout Nlumber Thlirteen. How he makee him for Linee. Makee Linee mally him. Sing he know what kindee fleaks Mlaxon makee. Linee always good to old Sing. Sing he been peeking thlu clack in wallee. See blig vlat where Thlirteen growing.

'Sing he takee you to Sing's shackee that night. Hide you till evlybody sleep. Then he sneak you in workee shop. Kickee over vlat. Leaves you. Nex' mlorning Mlaxon makee blig hulabaloo. Dance up and downee. Whoop! Thlirteen clome too soonee, but allight; him finee, perfec' man. Whoop!

'Anyway you heap better for Linee than one Mlaxon's fleaks,' he concluded, turning toward Bulan.

'You are lying, you yellow devil,' cried von Horn.

The Chinaman turned his shrewd, slant eyes malevolently upon the doctor.

'Sing lies?' he hissed. 'Mabbeso Sing lies when he ask what

for you glet Bludleen steal tleasure. But Lajah Saffir he come and spoil it all while you tly glet Linee to the ship – Sing knows.

'Then you tellee Mlaxon Thlirteen steal Linee. You lie then and you knew you lie. You lie again when Thlirteen savee Linee flom Olong Outang – you say you savee Linee.

'Then you make bad talkee with Lajah Saffir at long-house. Sing hear you all timee. You tly getee tleasure away from Dlyaks for your self. Then—'

'Stop!' roared von Horn. 'Stop! You lying yellow sneak, before I put a bullet in you.'

'Both of you may stop now,' said Professor Maxon authoritatively. 'There have been charges made here that cannot go unnoticed. Can you prove these things Sing?' he asked turning to the Chinaman.

'I plove much by Bludleen's lascar. Bludleen tell him all 'bout Hornee. I plove some more by Dyak chief at long-house. He know lots. Lajah Saffir tell him. It all tlue, Mlaxon.'

'And is it true about this man – the thing that you have told us is true? He is not one of those created in the laboratory?'

'No, Mlaxon. You no makee fine young man like Blulan – you know lat, Mlaxon. You makee One, Two, Thlee – all up to Twelve. All fleaks. You ought to know, Mlaxon, lat you can no makee a Blulan.'

During these revelations Bulan had sat with his eyes fixed upon the Chinaman. There was a puzzled expression upon his wan, blood-streaked face. It was as though he were trying to wrest from the inner temple of his consciousness a vague and tantalizing memory that eluded him each time that he felt he had it within his grasp – the key to the strange riddle that hid his origin.

The girl kneeled close beside him, one small hand in his. Hope and happiness had supplanted the sorrow in her face. She tore the hem from her skirt, to bandage the bloody furrow that creased the man's temple. Professor Maxon stood silently by, watching the loving tenderness that marked each deft, little movement of her strong, brown hands.

The revelations of the past few minutes had shocked the old man into stupefied silence. It was difficult, almost impossible, for him to believe that Sing had spoken the truth and that this man was not one of the creatures of his own creation; yet from the bottom of his heart he prayed that it might prove the truth, for he saw that his daughter loved the man with a love that would be stayed by no obstacle or bound by no man-made law or social custom.

The Chinaman's indictment of von Horn had come as an added blow to Professor Maxon, but it had brought its own supporting evidence in the flood of recollections it had induced in the professor's mind. Now he recalled a hundred chance incidents and conversations with his assistant that pointed squarely toward the man's disloyalty and villainy. He wondered that he had been so blind as not to have suspected his lieutenant long before.

Virginia had at last succeeded in adjusting her rude bandage and stopping the flow of blood. Bulan had risen weakly to his feet. The girl supported him upon one side, and Sing upon the other. Professor Maxon approached the little group.

'I do not know what to make of all that Sing has told us,' he said. 'If you are not Number Thirteen who are you? Where did you come from? It seems very strange indeed – impossible, in fact. However, if you will explain who you are, I shall be glad to – ah – consider – ah – permitting you to pay court to my daughter.'

'I do not know who I am,' replied Bulan. 'I had always thought that I was only Number Thirteen, until Sing just spoke. Now I have a faint recollection of drifting for days upon the sea in an open boat – beyond that all is blank. I shall not force my attentions upon Virginia until I can prove my identity, and that my past is one which I can lay before her without shame – until then I shall not see her.'

'You shall do nothing of the kind,' cried the girl. 'You love me, and I you. My father intended to force me to marry you while he still thought that you were a soulless thing. Now that it is quite apparent that you are a human being and a gentleman he hesitates, but I do not. As I have told you before, it makes no difference to me what you are. You have told me that you love me. You have demonstrated a love that is high, and noble, and self-sacrificing. More than that no girl needs to know. I am satisfied to be the wife of Bulan – if Bulan is satisfied to have the daughter of the man who has so cruelly wronged him.'

An arm went around the girl's shoulders and drew her close

to the man she had glorified with her loyalty and her love. The other hand was stretched out toward Professor Maxon.

'Professor,' said Bulan, 'in the face of what Sing has told us, in the face of a disinterested comparison between myself and the miserable creatures of your experiments, is it not folly to suppose that I am one of them? Some day I shall recall my past, until that time shall prove my worthiness I shall not ask for Virginia's hand, and in this decision she must concur, for the truth might reveal some insurmountable obstacle to our marriage. In the meantime let us be friends, professor, for we are both actuated by the same desire – the welfare and happiness of your daughter.'

The old man stepped forward and took Bulan's hand. The expression of doubt and worry had left his face.

'I cannot believe,' he said, 'that you are other than a gentleman, and if, in my desire to protect Virginia, I have said aught to wound you I ask your forgiveness.'

Bulan responded only with a tighter pressure of the hand.

'And now,' said the professor, 'let us return to the long-house. I wish to have a few words in private with you, von Horn,' and he turned to face his assistant, but the man had disappeared.

'Where is Doctor von Horn?' exclaimed the scientist, addressing Sing.

'Hornee, him vamoose long time 'go,' replied the Chinaman. 'He hear all he likee.'

Slowly the little party wound along the jungle trail, and in less than a mile, to Virginia's infinite surprise, came out upon the river and the long-house that she and Bulan had searched for in vain.

'And to think,' she cried, 'that all these awful days we have been almost within sound of your voices. What strange freak of fate sent you to us today?'

'We had about given up hope,' replied her father, 'when Sing suggested to me that we cut across the highlands that separate this valley from the one adjoining it upon the northeast, where we should strike other tribes and from them glean some clue to your whereabouts in case your abductors had attempted to carry you back to the sea by another route. This seemed likely in view of the fact that we were assured by enemies of Muda Saffir that you were not in his possession, and that the river we were bound for would lead your captors most quickly out of the domains of that rascally Malay. You may imagine our surprise, Virginia, when after proceeding for but a mile we discovered you.'

No sooner had the party entered the verandah of the long-house than Professor Maxon made inquiries for von Horn, only to learn that he had departed up stream in a prahu with several warriors whom he had engaged to accompany him on a 'hunting expedition', having explained that the white girl had been found and was being brought to the long-house.

The chief further explained that he had done his best to dissuade the white man from so rash an act, as he was going directly into the country of the tribe of the two men he had killed, and there was little chance that he ever would come out alive.

While they were still discussing von Horn's act, and wondering at his intentions, a native on the verandah cried out in astonishment, pointing down the river. As they looked in the direction he indicated all saw a graceful, white cutter gliding around a nearby turn. At the oars were white clad American sailors, and in the stern two officers in the uniform of the United States navy.

XVII

999 PRISCILLA

As the cutter touched the bank the entire party from the long-house, whites and natives, were gathered on the shore to meet it. At first the officers held off as though fearing a hostile demonstration, but when they saw the whites among the throng, a command was given to pull in, and a moment later one of the officers stepped ashore.

'I am Lieutenant May,' he said, 'of the *U.S.S. New Mexico*, flagship of the Pacific Fleet. Have I the honor to address Professor Maxon?'

The scientist nodded. 'I am delighted,' he said.

'We have been to your island, Professor,' continued the officer, 'and judging from the evidences of hasty departure, and the corpses of several natives there, I feared that some harm had befallen you. We therefore cruised along the Bornean coast making inquiries of the natives until at last we found one who had heard a rumor of a party of whites being far in the interior searching for a white girl who had been stolen from them by pirates.

'The farther up this river we have come the greater our assurance that we were on the right trail, for scarcely a native we interrogated but had seen or heard of some of your party. Mixed with the truth they told us were strange tales of terrible monsters led by a gigantic white man.'

'The imaginings of childish minds,' said the professor. 'However, why, my dear lieutenant, did you honor me by visiting my island?'

The officer hesitated a moment before answering, his eyes running about over the assembly as though in search of someone.

'Well, Professor Maxon, to be quite frank,' he said at length, 'we learned at Singapore the personnel of your party, which included a former naval officer whom we have been seeking for many years. We came to your island to arrest this man – I refer to Doctor Carl von Horn.'

When the lieutenant learned of the recent disappearance of the man he sought, he expressed his determination to push on at once in pursuit and as Professor Maxon feared again to remain unprotected in the heart of the Bornean wilderness his entire party was taken aboard the cutter.

A few miles up the river they came upon one of the Dyaks who had accompanied von Horn a few hours earlier. The warrior sat smoking beside a beached prahu. When interrogated he explained that von Horn and the balance of his crew had gone inland, leaving him to guard the boat. He said that he thought he could guide them to the spot where the white man might be found.

Professor Maxon and Sing accompanied one of the officers and a dozen sailors in the wake of the Dyak guide. Virginia and Bulan remained in the cutter, as the latter was still too weak to attempt the hard march through the jungle. For an hour the party traversed the trail in the wake of von Horn and his savage companions. They had come almost to the spot when their ears were assailed by the weird and blood curdling yells of native warriors, and a moment later von Horn's escort dashed into view in full retreat.

At sight of the white men they halted in relief, pointing back in the direction they had come, and jabbering excitedly in their native tongue. Warily the party advanced again behind these new guides; but when they reached the spot they sought, the cause of the Dyaks' panic had fled, warned, doubtless, by their trained ears of the approach of an enemy.

The sight that met the eyes of the searchers told all of the story that they needed to know. A hole had been excavated in the ground, partially uncovering a heavy chest, and across this chest lay the headless body of Doctor Carl von Horn.

Lieutenant May turned toward Professor Maxon with a questioning look.

'It is he,' said the scientist.

'But the chest?' inquired the officer.

'Mlaxon's tleasure,' spoke up Sing Lee. 'Hornee him tly steal it for long time.'

'Treasure!' ejaculated the professor. 'Bududreen gave up his life for this. Rajah Muda Saffir fought and intrigued and murdered for possession of it! Poor, misguided von Horn has died for it, and left his head to wither beneath the rafters of a Dyak long-house! It is incredible.'

'But, Professor Maxon,' said Lieutenant May, 'men will suffer all these things and more for gold.'

'Gold?' cried the professor. 'Why, man, that is a box of books on biology and eugenics.'

'My God!' exclaimed May, 'and von Horn was accredited to be one of the shrewdest swindlers and adventurers in America! But come, we may as well return to the cutter – my men will carry the chest.'

'No!' exclaimed Professor Maxon with a vehemence the other could not understand. 'Let them bury it again where it lies. It and what it contains have been the cause of sufficient misery and suffering and crime. Let it lie where it is in the heart of savage Borneo, and pray to God that no man ever finds it, and that I shall forget forever that which is in it.'

On the morning of the third day following the death of von Horn the *New Mexico* steamed away from the coast of Borneo. Upon her deck, looking back toward the verdure clad hills, stood Virginia and Bulan.

'Thank heaven,' exclaimed the girl fervently, 'that we are leaving it behind us forever.'

'Amen,' replied Bulan, 'but yet, had it not been for Borneo I might never have found you.'

'We should have met elsewhere then, Bulan,' said the girl in a low voice, 'for we were made for one another. No power on earth could have kept us apart. In your true guise you would have found me – I am sure of it.'

'It is maddening, Virginia,' said the man, 'to be constantly straining every resource of my memory in futile endeavor to catch and hold one fleeting clue to my past. Why, dear, do you realize that I may have been a fugitive from justice, as was von Horn, a vile criminal perhaps. It is awful, Virginia, to contemplate the horrible possibilities of my lost past.'

'No, Bulan, you could never have been a criminal,' replied the loyal girl, 'but there is one possibility that has been haunting me constantly. It frightens me just to think of it – it is,' and the girl lowered her voice as though she feared to say the thing she dreaded most, 'it is that you may have loved another – that – that you may even be married.'

Bulan was about to laugh away any such fears when the

154

gravity and importance of the possibility impressed him quite as fully as it had Virginia. He saw that it was not at all unlikely that he was already a married man; and he saw too what the girl now acknowledged, that they might never wed until the mystery of his past had been cleared away.

'There is something that gives weight to my fear,' continued Virginia, 'something that I had almost forgotten in the rush and excitement of events during the past few days. During your delirium your ravings were, for the most part, quite incoherent, but there was one name that you repeated many times – a woman's name, preceded by a number. It was "Nine ninety nine Priscilla". Maybe she—'

But Virginia got no further. With a low exclamation of delight Bulan caught her in his arms.

'It is all right, dear,' he cried. 'It is all right. Everything has come back to me now. You have given me the clue. Nine ninety nine Priscilla is my father's address – Nine ninety nine Priscilla Avenue.

'I am Townsend J. Harper, Jr. You have heard of my father. Every one has since he commenced consolidating interurban traction companies. And I'm not married, Virginia, and never have been; but I shall be if this miserable old mud scow ever reaches Singapore.'

'Oh, Bulan,' cried the girl, 'how in the world did you ever happen to come to that terrible island of ours?'

'I came for you, dear,' he replied. 'It is a long story. After dinner I will tell you all of it that I can recall. For the present it must suffice you to know that I followed you from the railway station at Ithaca half around the world for a love that had been born from a single glance at your sweet face as you passed me to enter your Pullman.

'On my father's yacht I reached your island after trailing you to Singapore. It was a long and tedious hunt and we followed many blind leads, but at last we came off an island upon which natives had told us such a party as yours was living. Five of us put off in a boat to explore – that is the last that I can recall. Sing says he found me alone in a row boat, a "dummy".'

Virginia sighed, and crept closer to him.

'You may be the son of the great Townsend J. Harper, you have been the soulless Number Thirteen; but to me you will always be Bulan, for it was Bulan whom I learned to love.'

155

Edgar Rice Burroughs

Three series by the Master of Imagination and Adventure

The exploits of David Innes in the perilous lands of the earth's core

Adventure in uncharted Caprona, a land of Dawn Age men and monsters

Universal warfare between moon-dwellers and the Earth of the far future

Occult and the Unusual

War

Westerns

"Alias Smith & Jones"—original novels of the famous outlaws

Dead Ringer Brian Fox	.. 35p
Outlaw Trail Brian Fox	.. 35p
Cabin Fever Brian Fox	.. 40p
Apache Gold Brian Fox	.. 40p
Trick Shot Brian Fox	.. 50p

"Dollar Westerns" featuring "The Man With No Name"

A Dollar To Die For Brian Fox	.. 30p
For a Few Dollars More Joe Millard..	.. 35p
The Good, The Bad, The Ugly Joe Millard	.. 35p
Blood For A Dirty Dollar Joe Millard	.. 30p
The Million Dollar Bloodhunt Joe Millard	.. 35p
A Coffin Full Of Dollars Joe Millard	.. 35p

"Spur Award" Westerns, Winners of the Coveted Prize

Outlaw Destiny Clifford Adams	.. 45p
Tragg's Choice Clifford Adams	.. 45p
The White Man's Road Benjamin Capps	.. 50p
The Saber Brand Herbert Purdum	.. 50p
The Red Sabbath Lewis B. Patten	.. 45p

Name...

Address..

Titles required..

....

....

....

....

....

....
